Sullivan Productions Presents

I0632909

A Novel by Best Selling Author
LEO SULLIVAN

SULLIVAN
PRODUCTIONS

Acknowledgments

First and foremost, I would like to thank God for blessing me with a gift to touch other people's lives with the stroke of a pen.

I would also like to thank my family and friends, who are too many to name. Besides, I always get in trouble when I forget that one person. Not this time.

With this project, it was special because of the people who were so instrumental from the book's first inception. I had to call on my dude, Cash, a national bestselling author, for his sagacious insight into the netherworld of gangsterism. Thanks, my brotha. Also, I'd be remiss if I didn't show mad love to the extraordinarily talented author Jennifer Luckett. She was also instrumental in the development of this project. Her feminine insight into the mentality of a young girl was profound. Whenever I ran into a problem, she was the first person I called. She also helped with editing.

Okay, let me introduce you to the members of the band: The beautiful and very multifaceted Renee Camile. That's always her melodious sound you hear on social media sites such as Facebook and other mediums to make sure my books get promoted. She does a great job. Then you have the fan/Fam, YOU. Without your harmonious melody and staunch support, there would be no music. I would be like a singer without a voice, an actor without an audience. Your love and support are what push me forward to be the best damn author I can be. I don't write for the love of money; I write for the love of writing.

Next, my band will be playing an erotic tune called Billionairess Thief. It's erotica, and it's a banger. Don't forget to write a review and buy some books from my website. LeoLSullivan.com

Okay, I'ma keep it gangsta!

I'm out.

Leo L. Sullivan

Prologue

The sound of hospital machines beeped and drummed in my head in a melody of gloom. I lay in the ICU at The University of Miami Hospital in a semi-conscious state, somewhere between alive and traumatized to the point of wanting to be dead. I could feel the blood-soaked bandages tightly wrapped around my head. I could also faintly hear voices around me, but I could not make out who they belonged to. I strained to open my eyes, but they were swollen shut.

What happened soon flashed back through my mind in frightening photos. I shuddered at the images. In order to block out the gruesomeness of what flashed behind my closed eyelids, I summoned up snapshots of prettier events the day before the tragedy. It was the weekend of the high school prom, and life seemed happy and trouble-free. Daddy surprised me with the best graduation gift of my life!

I screamed with excitement the moment I saw it. It was a dream come true.

Then, devastation quickly tore our lives apart. Killers in ski masks terrorized us. At the time, I didn't realize that things would turn out the way they had. The consequences of what occurred would surely mean death for the culprits. Slain bodies would be everywhere before it was over and done. There was about to be a war in the streets, and I wasn't afraid to lay down for my family.

Tears ran down my face.

Where are you, Daddy? Are you still alive? There was so much blood and trauma. I whimpered as I remembered all of the carnage and bloodshed. What happened to Ike Jr.? I tried to recall, but it was difficult. There was so much carnage left inside our home.

"Who did this, Kadisha?" The sound of an officious voice cut through the gruesome images in my mind.

I didn't respond, but a face appeared in my memory. The face of one of the men changed my life forever. That face had forever turned me cold. The sheltered schoolgirl was gone, and in her place was A Gangster's Daughter, who was out for payback. Punishment was no longer the Almighty Father's job. Hell naw! I intended to serve street justice to whoever did this to us. First, I had to overcome my injuries, and then it would be hell in the streets. I prayed that God would help me. Once I recuperated, my enemies would need the help of God and all his angels. That wasn't just a threat. It was a promise!

CHAPTER
One

Miami, Florida

On that sunny day, the world seemed to pass by as I daydreamed. A million thoughts entered my young mind. The chatter of my little sister, Keona, and Daddy's voice murmured in the background. I sat in the backseat of his 2012 brick-red Mercedes Benz G-Class SUV, thinking. My life had been unpredictable and full of many twists, turns, and surprises. That's how I became the young woman I am.

Normally, Keona and I would have argued over the front seat, or I would have strong-armed it. That day was different. This was to be 'our' day, my daddy had declared. Ironically, Keona's birthday fell on the same day that I graduated from college. I was smart as a whip and graduated with cum laude honors. Thank God, I was blessed with brains. When I was in the fourth grade, I was so intelligent that I was promoted to the sixth grade that same year. That made my father proud.

My mother had turned her back and walked away from us. She didn't even have enough decency to show up to my graduation. That hurt me to my soul. Anyway, during my sophomore year in high school, my father encouraged me to take online classes. That's when I earned my associate's degree. Some of the most prestigious schools offered me several academic scholarships. Harvard and Yale were a few well-known names among many.

My dream was to become a surgeon. However, Daddy was adamant that I go to a historically black college. He felt that America chose the most brilliant African-American minds from the ghetto and offered them opportunities at their universities. Daddy believed that the students' minds would become like Europeans. They served no purpose to their communities. Not only did he say they thought they were white, but they talked and acted white, too. Which, he was right in many ways because those graduates would not come back to the hoods and support their communities. They would use their huge incomes to support Caucasians and forget where they came from.

I ended up being accepted to Florida A&M University. I was so thrilled, and so was he. Daddy had his mind set on me running his business one day. He owned Ike's One Stop Grocery, located in Liberty City. He also owned Ike's Detail Shop, located across the street from the grocery store. Actually, when he was younger, he would hustle out of the detail Shop. He invested his money in real estate. I was shocked when he continued to prosper even after the market crashed. My daddy's name is Ike Spencer, and his life is a true rags-to-riches hood legend story...

The streets know as they always do when one of their own climbs out of the unpleasantness of anguish and sits on a throne in the height of Miami's notoriously violent drug trade. He started out as a corner hustler, selling crack and weed in the projects. A fourteen-year-old father who was in the streets and caught up in the vicious drug wars, he quickly earned the infamous nickname "Monster." Actually, a police lieutenant named him that after a violent series of grisly murders.

In one incident, three rivals lost their lives in broad daylight, execution style, and their comrades were plowed down with an AK-47 at a funeral as they carried the casket of their dead homie. Mourners looked on. The same crew had also murdered the man in the casket. Lieutenant Basdin went on national television and said that my father, Ike Spencer, was a suspect in the vicious killings and that only a monster could do such a despicable and hideous act. From that day forward, both friends and foes called Daddy "Monster." By then, the streets were caught up in the vicious yoke of Miami's gangland violence and its illicit drug trade.

During those years, Miami led the nation in two categories: the most seizures of cocaine ever captured and homicides. Rumors spread that Daddy organized a crew of killers called The Booby Boys. They were young gangsters who killed over territory and control of the drug trade. Eerily, I remembered on more than one occasion that my mother and I would be terrified as we watched the news. The slain bodies were scattered in the streets, at clubs, and gas stations. They dealt with the enemy wherever they caught them slipping. Mama knew many of the victims, and she would always cry. In my mind, I knew the murders had something to do with my father. I think my mother was afraid of my Daddy. I often believed that he was the main reason she left.

Recently, the rapper Rick Ross was doing some name calling in one of his songs and mentioned Daddy's name. I was ecstatic about it. However, Daddy was furious when I told him about it. He thought about serving Ross a courtesy call in person. He said name-dropping was a violation and disrespectful. My father had been out of the game for years. Most of his old crew were either dead or serving life sentences in the feds. Daddy now lived his life as a reputable businessman. He even attended church regularly, mentored troubled youth, and had a youth basketball team called the Junior Miami Heat. My baby brother, Ike Jr., was on the team. I was the assistant coach. We had a blast. Daddy had become a great role model for the community.

I SHOULD HAVE BEEN happy that day, but I wasn't. Something was deeply troubling my father, and that affected me as well. Every so often, I'd catch him looking out the window as if he were waiting for something to happen. Also, I'd noticed Big Bee's pearl-white Escalade truck trailing us when we left the mall. That also disturbed me. Big Bee was like an uncle to me. He was a bear of a man. He stood six feet eight and weighed over three hundred pounds. He had a violent reputation in the streets for putting in work. Some thought he was involved in the brutal murder of Clay Jackson. Jackson was a dopeboy from Goulds, Florida. He and my father had been beefing hard.

Clay saw my mother at a shopping mall one Saturday. He walked up and pimp slapped her. He then threatened to fire off on my father when he caught him slipping. She was five months pregnant with my little brother at the time. Three weeks later, Mama and I were walking to the corner store. We spotted Clay with his two small kids, about to walk into the barbershop. Suddenly, a green four-door Buick LaSabre drove by and opened fire. Me and Mama fell to the ground. Several bullets flew through the barbershop, struck three cars, and barely missed hitting the two small children.

Clay jumped in the line of fire to protect his kids. He grabbed them, dropped to the ground, and the assailants fired bullets into his back. I had an expression of utter shock and felt grief for those kids. Big Bee was a suspect in that slaying.

The next day, there were bullet holes and crime scene

tape on the door of the barbershop. The whole incident would scar me for the rest of my life.

I remember a time when I overheard Big Bee and my daddy masterminding a heist in which the two of them robbed a shipment of coke from some Cubans. The drugs were in a cargo boat, concealed in barrels of coffee that was on the port of Miami's dock. I was about eight years old then. That, too, resulted in many drug wars with Daddy's crew, The Booby Boys, and the Cubans.

This day, Big Bee was acting like a bodyguard. Daddy strangely continued to look out the window with a strange expression.

I began to ramble through the shopping bag of items I had purchased from Macy's. One of them was a Louis Vuitton purse and matching boots, which Daddy had bought for my graduation. The purse and shoes cost over a stack, along with the other accessories I bought.

"Kadisha, baby, I'm sorry your mom couldn't make it to your graduation," Daddy said in a soft voice filled with sympathy. He made eye contact with me in the rearview mirror. I saw the hurt in his eyes, but I also saw something else as he scanned the cars that passed us.

My little sister, Keona, had the radio turned up loud. One of Chris Brown's songs was on, and she sang along merrily. She was dancing and popping her fingers to the beat with the youthfulness of her adolescence. Normally, Daddy would have turned the radio down, but that day, he didn't.

"Oh, it's okay. Mama probably had better things to do," I responded to my daddy with sarcasm. He gave me a sympathetic nod as he drove. I added, "Besides, I know she's probably somewhere getting high."

Daddy looked at me begrudgingly through the rearview mirror with a frown as his brown eyes sought to comfort me. Keona seemed to be oblivious to my mom's absence. She had good reason to be because she was only five years old when Mama just up and left us. On the other hand, I was ten, and by then, my mom had made a big impression on me.

Not only was Mama a mother to me, she was my best friend. She was everything I needed. She and my father had been childhood sweethearts. They grew up in Miami's notorious Pork and Beans projects. I didn't know what happened. I did know that, at the time, she had started experimenting with drugs recreationally by snorting cocaine. At first, Daddy was unaware of her new habit.

One day, I came home from school, and without saying a word, my mother had packed a few of her belongings and was gone. I was sure Daddy's lifestyle and all the murders he was involved in had also led to her leaving. Another reason could have been that she was a 'cokehead.' She had abandoned us. At the time, my baby brother was an infant. I knew it was hard on my daddy. It hurt him to the core. That was the only time I ever saw him, with his eyes filled with tears.

It wasn't a major secret that my father was a hustler. I had seen him stash money and guns in my mattress when I was a little girl. Once, the police raided our apartment in the projects. I was in bed sick with the flu the entire time. They never found the guns.

Mama would talk as if I was an adult. Maybe it was because we had so much in common. She was a child raising a child in the heart of the ghetto. My mom was thirteen when she had me, and my father was a year older. He was a child who had to become a man. He always told me that he would get us out of the projects. It took years and a lot of blood, sweat, and tears. I mean blood literary, but he did it. Secretly, he wanted me to be a boy, and I was sort of. We did so much stuff together.

When he was younger, he would take me to the basketball court with him, and I'd watch him hoop. That had a big effect on me. I ended up becoming a tomboy. I loved to play basketball; it was my favorite sport. Back in the day, we'd go to the Miami Heat games. I'd sit courtside amongst the celebrities in three thousand dollar seats and root for Dwayne Wade and King James. Once, we sat right next to Baby of Cash Money. There were so many celebrities at those games. I still love it to this day.

Daddy is the person who taught me how to shoot a gun. He often took me and my sister to the shooting range. Keona really didn't care for guns. On the other hand, I adored the feel of the nine-millimeter's cold steel in my hands. I could make a gun pop off with accuracy, reload it, and shoot some more.

The most valuable lesson that I learned from my daddy

was about boys. He told me everything I needed to know about the opposite sex. Like most dads, he didn't want me to have intercourse. He said that whenever I chose to be with a man, I should always use protection. He'd rather tell me that than risk me having unprotected sex in the back seat of some boy's car and getting pregnant or catching a disease. After all, Daddy was a street dude and an ex-goon. He knew how it went down in the streets, and he'd kick me some knowledge. He didn't sugarcoat anything. He always kept it real. That was one of the things I admired about him.

WE SOON PULLED into our luxurious home in Palmetto Bay. My eyes were glued to something beautiful parked in the driveway. It was a candy-apple red BMW 360 Convertible Sports Coupe wrapped in a huge red bow. I completely lost it. I jumped out before the vehicle could stop. Ms. Shay, our elderly Asian housekeeper, was watering the lawn when I frightened her. I was running and screaming like one of those happy chicks from The Price Is Right who had just won a new car. Ms. Shay looked like she almost jumped out of her skin at first. She placed her hand over the left side of her chest. My little brother, Ike Jr., stopped playing and stared at me with a smile.

I frantically raced around the car and opened the door.

The new car smell filled my nostrils. Factory plastic covered the leather seats. Everyone walked over with huge smiles covering their faces. However, my father had the biggest grin. He had surprised me, and he knew it.

"Thank you, Daddy! Oh, my God!" I jumped into his arms.

Our playful white pit bull with a brown patch over his left eye yapped at my heels. The festive mood became even happier as my sister, Keona, ran over and jumped into the passenger's seat, mouth wide open, like she was more shocked than I was. My little badass brother got into the car and pretended to be driving while blowing the horn.

"Now, I know you didn't think I was going to send my baby girl off to college without a nice ride." Daddy proudly beamed.

I hugged him again while burying my face in the crook of his neck. I fought back joyful tears.

Big Bee strolled up behind me. He, too, had a mischievous smile on his face when he extended his hand and said, "Kadisha, here's something to hold you over in case you ever need some extra cash." He handed me a fat envelope full of money and then smothered me with a big hug in his massive arms.

I thanked him with a soft whisper. I was too choked up to speak. Then, my seven-year-old brother and my sister went into their juvenile antics and began to chant at the same time.

"We want to go for a ride."

The dog was barking as he jumped onto the backseat of the car.

As Keona admired the plush interior, she chimed, "I want you to teach me how to drive. Come on, Kadisha." She reached over and turned the key in the ignition. Travis Porter's music played. "Ride Like That," featuring Jeremih, blasted through the Alpine stereo.

Daddy became slightly agitated.

He said, "Okay, everybody out the car! I need to make a phone call first to the insurance agency. I had the car rushed here. I want to double-check the policy and be sure that it's covered under the best policy available."

I somberly pouted. I was ready to get into my new whip, go pick my girls up, and bust some blocks. Daddy knew I was upset. He pulled me to the side, lovingly placed his hand on my shoulder, and smiled at me.

"Baby girl, I know you've been stressing about some things for the past few months. I know that you're worried about going off to college. I'm sorry that your mom isn't here to help you. I also know that I haven't always done the right things. Stop worrying. As a parent, my job is to make sure you don't want for anything, to love you, and to take care of you. Your job is simply to be happy, have fun, go to school, be responsible, and continue to get good grades."

"I am happy, Daddy," I replied. I looked up and spotted a blimp floating in the fluffy blue clouds.

"Lately, it seems like you've been stressed out about

things. You don't have to be. Everything is good; just look around you." He proudly spread his arms.

Just that fast, my father had soothed my apprehension by telling me things I didn't even realize were troubling me. Truth be told, when Mama left, I took the lead in taking care of the family. I made sure that my little brother had clean clothes and that my sister did her homework. I even listened to my daddy when he needed somebody to talk to. Right then, I decided to stop worrying so much and just enjoy my life as my daddy insisted. Maybe I needed to go to the beach and watch the waves splash and chill. I needed some *me* time.

I should have been happy, though, because Daddy bought a five-bedroom, four-bath home in the wealthy Palmetto area of Miami. Most of our neighbors were Cuban, white, and a few aristocratic blacks. Really, I think one of the reasons he purchased the home was because it was in a cul-de-sac. It was a secluded area at the end of the block. The beautiful two-story brick home reminded me of the ones I'd seen on MTV Cribs. The house had all the amenities: a heated inside swimming pool, a basketball court, a Jacuzzi, and a gym. We were living the good life for the time being, but a catastrophe would eventually knock on our door and end it all.

CHAPTER
Two

Kadisha

D addy kissed my forehead, and I watched as he and Big Bee walked over to Bee's Escalade. The two of them chatted for a moment. When I heard my daddy's laughter, I felt at peace with the world. The thoughts in my head drifted back to my shiny new car. My sister walked over toward me. I heard Big Bee tell my daddy that he was going to the store and would be back in a minute. Daddy waved at him and walked by to enter the house. Ike Jr., Ms. Shay, and the dog followed him into the house. The dog was wagging his tail. That's when I heard my little brother ask Daddy if he could get a car for his birthday. My sister, Keona, and I cracked up in laughter.

Lately, I had been somewhat mean to my sister. She could get on my last nerve as a younger sibling often does. If she wasn't asking to wear my clothes, she was snitching on me or trying to run behind me every place I went.

She fidgeted when she asked, "Kadisha, can you take me for a ride after Daddy gets the insurance thing worked out. Please?" I felt bad for how I had been treating her lately.

"Yeah, you can go. We'll go back to the mall and do some shopping. I'll get you the iPhone you wanted for your birthday," I said and opened the envelope Big Bee had given me. Nothing but one-hundred-dollar bills was inside.

Her eyes bucked wide as I peeled off three and gave them to her.

"Thank you! Thank you!" she caroled excitedly and then added, "Okay, let me go change clothes."

Keona ran into the house, and I was left alone with my thoughts. I strolled over to my car. The sunlight from the bright sun gleamed off the hood. Suddenly, my mood was disturbed. I looked up and saw my boyfriend, Steve's Camry come to a stop in the driveway. He bounced out of the car with his shoulder-length dreads swaying. He had on blue jeans, a crisp white T-shirt, and Air Force Ones.

"Wassup, Kadisha?" Before I could answer, he added, "Damn, somebody got a raw ass gift." He toyed with the red bow wrapped around the car.

"It's fiyah, ain't it? Daddy gave it to me for graduation," I proudly said with a smile that stretched from one ear to the other. I could hardly contain my joy.

"Get out of here!" He gave me a side glance out the corner of his eye to see if I was playing.

"You'll see tonight when you come to pick me up for the prom," I confidently retorted.

He got into the driver's seat and ran his hands over the wood grain and leather interior.

"I'm driving!" He impishly smiled.

I shook my head. "No, you ain't."

"It's prom night. I'm the chauffeur. How is it going to look with you driving me around?"

I gave what he said some consideration. He did have a point. Then he added, "Afterwards, we're going to get a room at the Regency. You gon' lemme hit it, and then you'll officially be my ol' lady." He smiled mischievously while intentionally licking his lips. The wide hips that I'd been blessed with caught his attention. He stood there eyeballing me like my banging body had him in a trance.

Steve had an outstanding swag, and he knew it. I was attracted to him at first because he was tall and had an athletic build. He had a cinnamon complexion with freckles on his face. His hair was sandy red, and he had hazel eyes. For some reason, my daddy liked him a lot. Steve would come over and run odd errands for Daddy. Nevertheless, I had my suspicions about that.

I had the biggest crush on Steve during my freshman year. He played point guard for Miami High. They made it all the way to the semifinals that year. He was a sophomore and very good at sports. All the girls were attracted to him, including me. Luckily, I was the one who captured his heart.

We were the perfect example that opposites really do attract.

I am a deep chocolate brown with naturally long, curly hair that flows down my back. I have a nice hourglass figure with a slim waist. My breasts are small, but I make up for them with my backside. My hips are curvaceous and thick. My butt got me a lot of attention in school, and I loved it. However, once I entered high school, boys would walk behind me and flirtatiously check me out when I wore tight jeans or a short skirt. It took a while to learn how to deal with all the attention. After a while, I got used to it. That was a plus for me. Most men wanted a woman with a bubble butt. I would often catch Steve looking at me and smiling as I passed him in the hallway. I couldn't help but blush. I was sure he got a big kick out of my schoolgirl crush. The thing was, I didn't know how to get him.

One day, I was sitting in the cafeteria, eating with my girls, Latoya and Shamika, when Steve walked in with some of his boys. Latoya was a sophomore. She had all the boys eating out of her hand. She was pretty with a caramel complexion, long legs, and thick in all the right places. She nudged me under the table with her elbow.

"Gurl, there he is! You better get his ass."

I looked up to see Steve. He was so fine. He made my heart flutter. It felt like I was going to hyperventilate. To make matters worse, I was so shy. I wanted to cover my face and hide under the table.

"I... I don't know what to do," I stuttered during my response.

"Gurl, just smile at him when he looks your way. Call him with your eyes like this." Latoya batted her pretty eyelashes and smiled. Then, she seductively glided her tongue over her pouty lips. She was being silly with the last move. We all burst out laughing.

I did what she suggested, except for the tongue part. It worked like a charm. Steve and his boys swaggered over to our table and sat down without even asking. I thought I was going to die, but it all worked out fine. He was smooth and very nice. We kicked it and had a good time. He actually made me laugh a lot. Afterward, he asked for my phone number. Of course, I gave it to him. My girls, Latoya and Shamika, ended up going out with his friends.

Steve soon dropped out of school, and I started hearing rumors that he had a chick on the side. I also heard that he was involved with some shiesty people who had been stealing cars and doing petty robberies. As time passed, I started to see another side of him. He was soft as cotton, and I would run all over him. I would have even had sex with him. For years, he had been begging for some coochie. All he had to do was just take it.

I was attracted to roughneck dudes with that thug appearance and swag. I figured I wouldn't have to tell thugs what to do. The ones who would know that sometimes no meant yes. I would only let him fondle my breasts and ass. That really turned me on. A couple of times, I even let him go down on me. Therefore, it was all good. I was still a virgin.

"No, you will not be making me a woman officially." Then, out of spite, I added, "Maybe you should talk to my daddy about making me a woman tonight," I kidded and watched his cheeks flush red.

"Come on, girl, stop playing." He reached into his pocket, pulled out a huge bankroll, and sheepishly smiled. He tried to grab my waist.

"I ain't playing, boy." I swatted at his hand and moved out of reach.

Something was so uncharacteristic about him that day. For one, he never had money, but he was suddenly flaunting a chunk of cash.

"Seriously, is your daddy in the house?" He had turned serious.

"Yeah, why? He is not going to let you drive my car." I giggled.

"Naw, I just wanted to know if he was here."

Just then, my little brother and the dog ran out into the yard. For some reason, my little badass brother didn't like boys talking to me, especially Steve. No matter how hard Steve tried to win his approval.

Ike Jr. and the dog wasted no time running up to Steve.

"What's up, little man?" Steve playfully said.

"Nigga, get out my yard fo' I sic Plato on you."

"I'm telling Daddy. Go back in the house, boy!" I yelled at my little brother.

Steve tried to play it off with a grin and asked, "Little man, why you don't like m—" Before he could get the word out his mouth, my brother taunted.

"Get him, Plato!" To my surprise, the dog began to crawl and bark menacingly, snapping at Steve's leg and causing him to jump out of the way.

"I'ma beat yo' little ass!" I took off chasing after him. The whole time, he was laughing as we ran with the dog barking behind us.

As we reached the front of the yard, I heard the pulsating sound of music blaring. The rapper 2 Chainz's "Birthday Song" was playing. "All I want for my birthday is a big booty ho..."

I looked up to see a candy-painted money-green '64 Chevy convertible rolling on twenty-fours coming up the street. The car looked familiar as I squinted in the bright sunlight. I had to do a double-take as it neared. It was none other than Mellow. The last time I had seen him or his tricked-out Chevy was about a year ago, at school.

Mellow had gone to prison for selling drugs. He was busted with a whole kilo. His sister, Keller, was in my first period class. She told me everything. Mellow told her to give me his prison address and asked me to write him. I wrote him a few times and even sent him some pictures. The truth was, Mellow was a thug to the tenth power. I would intentionally act stuck up when he spoke to me at school. Once, he grabbed my arm in the hallway in front of everybody and wouldn't let go. His ass was bold. I pretended like I was mad, but secretly, I liked his gangsta.

I had to act my part because all the girls liked him. He had an ill whip and dressed really nice. He was also cute with dimples. He was the first dude that I'd ever seen in Miami with a platinum and diamond grill in his mouth. He looked like the rapper T.I., but he was skinny as a beanpole. I played hard to get until I started writing him. Then, I explained why.

In one of the letters, I told him how I really felt and that I had a boyfriend. He and Steve could never get along. It was geographically impossible. Mellow was from Overtown, a rough side of Miami. Steve was from Liberty City. They were official goons over there as well. The two sections had been beefing with each other for years. It went back to my father's days of running the streets.

I could hardly catch my breath as the Chevy parked in front of my house, and Mellow hopped out. He had gained a lot of weight while he was away. He had on a white wife beater. His muscles glistened as they flexed in the sunlight. I could tell he must have been working out a lot. *What the hell they feeding them dudes in prison?* I thought as I looked over at Steve. I knew there was going to be a problem. I couldn't believe that Mellow had the audacity to show up at my house. Even though I wrote him while he was in prison, in no way did I give him the impression that we were going to be together when he got out. In fact, I told him about Steve.

Two of Mellow's homeboys sat in the car, watching

intensely as if something was about to pop off. I looked over my shoulder, and Steve started acting nervous by putting his hands in his pocket. Even my little brother sensed trouble. Before Mellow reached me, the potent scent of weed hit my nose.

"What's up, Kadisha?" Mellow spoke with an attitude, but he wasn't even looking at me. His attention was focused on Steve as he brushed right by me.

"Nigga, you know Bell got whacked last night after he left you," Mellow said, placing his hand in his waistband onto his strap. His chest bumped Steve.

The drama was unfolding so fast that I almost peed in my pants.

"M... man, I heard about that," Steve stuttered and started looking around like he was thinking about running.

"Nigga, what I'm hearing is you sold him a brick, took his muhfuckin' money, and didn't come back. They killed him sitting in his ride in front of the pool hall waiting on you."

Mellow was raging. I could see a protruding vein in his forehead. His muscles bulged, coiling like ropes underneath the thin t-shirt.

"Man, on er'thang I love, I didn't have nothing to do with th—"

Before Steve could get the statement out of his mouth, Mellow grabbed him around the collar and yanked him close. "Fuck nigga, you lying. Where that muhfuckin' money at, nigga?"

The Chevy doors opened. It was about to be Chopper City in the front yard. It was 'bout to go down. Mellow's boys stepped out of the vehicle. I could see the burners in their pants. They mean-mugged Steve, and one of the taller goons pushed him. From their expressions, I could tell that they were fully intent on slaughtering him. They were concealing some long guns that I guessed had to be AK-47s.

"Y'all, stop it, please!" I heard myself scream as I stepped back, nearly falling.

I reached for my little brother and held him in my arms. I was horrified. I felt like I was standing in front of an automobile that had no brakes. This was a tragedy waiting to happen. There was no way I could intervene. I had seen the damage that an AK-47 could do firsthand. I needed to get out of the way. A bullet had no name on it.

Mellow reached inside Steve's pocket and removed a large roll of cash. He then bitch slapped Steve's face before he removed his chrome-plated nine from his waistline and shoved it into Steve's side.

"Please, man," Steve begged. His voice trembled with what sounded like lots of fear.

"Go in the house," Mellow yelled at me as he held Steve around the shirt collar, fully intent on killing him in my front yard.

I had seen this before. Mellow didn't have to tell me twice. I took off running with my little brother in tow as the dog followed. I had to save my life and my brother's because things were about to get real ugly.

CHAPTER *Three*

Kadisha

Ms. Shay just happened to walk out the front door. Naïve to urban violence, she didn't even realize that she was putting her life in jeopardy. She could've become a victim of homicide.

"Y'all get out the yard with all the noise!"

Surprised, Mellow looked up and saw her. He quickly stashed the gun back into his waistband while his dudes ducked back into the Chevy.

"Yes, Ma'am," Mellow responded politely while eyeballing Steve with a murderous objective.

"Kadisha!" Mellow called my name, causing me to stop in my tracks. I could feel my right leg trembling as I turned around and looked at him.

"This nigga is rotten! Rotten to the core. Tell your

daddy don't fuck wit' this nigga. He ain't right." Mellow made a closed fist and socked Steve in the nose with a right hook.

"Come on, man," Steve nervously said. He looked like he wanted to cry as he took a step back. That was when I noticed a trickle of blood coming from his nose. He held up his palms as if to ward off the next blow.

"Nigga, I know where your mama and little sister live in Liberty City," Mellow threatened. He patted his waist where the burner was.

Ms. Shay had heard enough; she could sense something was wrong.

"Leave, get off the property," she said as she walked toward them.

Mellow bowed his head at her, but he continued to send Steve silent threats.

"Nigga, your ass is a wrap."

With that said, Mellow got back in the car with his dudes and mashed out. I exhaled a deep breath. It suddenly felt like all the energy had drained from my body.

I cut my eyes over at Steve just as Ms. Shay said, "Y'all come into this house. Your father is on the phone in his study. I am going to tell him."

"No! Don't tell him. I'll be inside in a minute," I said to Ms. Shay, trying to soothe her with my eyes.

She shook her head wearily and walked away. My little brother took the opportunity to tease Steve.

"You so scared that you doodooed in yo' pants," he mocked.

That was it! I had enough of his childish antics. I popped him upside his head. I felt like taking my belt off and whooping that ass. He tried to kick me and then ran inside the house crying, threatening to tell Daddy.

A flock of geese flew overhead as the sun beamed down on us. Steve began to pace the lawn. He suddenly became emboldened by Mellow's absence and began to rant. Instantly, he started to look so generic to me. It was as if I was seeing him as a wimp and a straight pussy.

"That nigga lucky I didn't have my Glock on me, or I would have burnt his punk ass up. You see, they had to come at a nigga three deep!" He wiped the blood running from his nose with the back of his hand as he looked at me to co-sign what he said.

Maybe I should have had sympathy for him because he was my guy, but I didn't. I saw a serious flaw in his character. It wasn't simply the fact that Mellow had bitched him up, slapped him, and took his money. It was what Mellow said that added to what had transpired. Mellow had planted a seed of serious doubt in my mind.

Steve stopped pacing, reached into his sock, and pulled out a neat stack of hundred-dollar bills.

"Stupid ass niggaz didn't even get all the money," he said while chuckling. His teeth were stained with blood as he waved the money at me. His eyes told a different story, however. I thought I detected something evil. It was strange.

Had he forgotten all about the dangers that lurked? Some niggaz had just shown up at my doorstep and was about to murder him and possibly me too.

"What time you want me to come by and pick you up for the prom?" Steve was jittery. He kept looking up the street as if he was waiting for something. He must have thought the dudes might come back.

"Don't come pick me up for the prom," I replied with animosity.

"Don't come? What do you mean, don't come?" he repeated, moving his mouth like he had suddenly gotten lockjaw.

"I ain't getting caught up in none of that bullshit. All of a sudden, you got money you ain't ever had," I spat.

"Oh. You gon' believe that soft ass nigga, Mell, over me?" Steve huffed and walked up close.

I glanced at the front door to be sure my daddy didn't come out. That was the last thing I needed.

"I'm just sayin', I don't want no drama in my life. You know Mellow is a problem. They were getting ready to kill you."

"That nigga ain't shit. He got me fucked up with some-body else. You believe all the bullshit he was saying?" Steve asked with his top lip snarled as he looked at me in search of an answer. I gave him a slight shrug. For some reason, I couldn't look him in the eye when I responded. He seemed lame to me. One thing I didn't want was a soft ass nigga up behind me.

"I don't know, but I will say this was too close to home and my family. I'm about to go off to college. Don't you understand?" I found myself pouting as my voice screeched. I stomped my feet.

He looked up the street and saw something that caught his attention. He glanced down at his watch and muttered under his breath. I think he called me a bitch. I wasn't sure. He turned and walked off. I felt like he was going to get a gun. In my heart, I knew that he would need it. I felt a sense of relief when he was gone.

I MOPED over and sat inside my new whip. The heat was soaring inside the vehicle. The leather seat sizzled my legs. I made a mental note to get the windows tinted as I watched the front door, expecting my daddy to come out at any minute. This was definitely not the way I intended to spend my prom weekend.

I had a bright idea to go for a ride around the block, even though I knew my daddy would kill me.

Maybe not.

Just as I was about to turn the key in the ignition, I happened to look in the review mirror and saw the white postal service van pull into the driveway and park.

"Package for Mr. Ike Spencer," the mail carrier said as he hopped out.

The front door of our house opened, and Plato and my little brother came running out. I didn't know what it was about dogs and postal workers, but Plato was going crazy, barking and growling at the mailman.

"Boy, go put that damn dog up!" I cursed at my little brother. He had gotten on my last nerve.

Ike Jr. grabbed the dog just as the mail carrier walked up. I volunteered to take the package. The mail carrier replied, "Sorry, but Mr. Spencer has to personally sign for the package."

Plato continued to bark and growl.

"Just a minute. Let me get my daddy," I said and attempted to grab the dog. My little brother ran into the house ahead of me, and Plato followed, still barking.

"I told Daddy you hit me, and he gon' get you," Ike Jr. said.

"Boy, get out my face!" I shoved him to the side and continued to walk. His little bad ass hit me in my back and took off running.

"Ouch!"

I walked into my daddy's nicely decorated study. His huge desk was mahogany brown and ivory. Paintings of ancient African kings and both nude and semi-nude queens adorned the walls. The scent of jasmine always seemed to heighten my senses.

My daddy was sitting at his desk when I walked in. His

head bowed as he busied himself going over some paperwork.

"Daddy, the mailman has a package he wants you to sign for," I said.

He looked up, startled, with music playing in the background. There were piles of miscellaneous papers on his desk, a neat stack of money, and cigar smoke coming from the astray. He seemed distressed. Stress had already caused him to age. He looked ten years older than his actual age.

"What did I tell you about hitting on your little brother? And what's going on with you and Steve? You two arguing again?"

"No, Daddy. They are all just getting on my nerves," I admitted.

As he passed, he gave my shoulders a gentle squeeze.

"Be good now. This is your special day. In addition, the insurance agency said all the papers are in order. You can drive the car anytime you're ready."

"Thank you, Daddy." I was all excited and could barely contain my joy.

"Did Big Bee make it back from the store yet?" he asked over his shoulder before he exited the study.

"No," I responded and watched him walk out.

For some reason, I just stood there in his study. That's when I heard Plato barking again. It was fiercer that time like there was scuffling or something going on. Then, I heard a gunshot that sent chills down my spine.

I took off running at full speed toward the sound of the

shots. I entered the kitchen and bumped into Ms. Shay. She had been vacuuming in the living room. My sister Keona was behind her. To my horror, the postal worker stood with three other men. They all had on ski masks and were armed with pistols. Plato lay on the floor, panting in a puddle of blood.

CHAPTER Four

Kadisha

"Everybody still, and don't no muthafuckin' body move!" one of the gunmen said.

He was tall and slender, dressed in a black Nike sweatsuit and white sneakers. I could only see the whites of his eyes and the gold grill in his mouth as he aimed his gun at my daddy's chest. The other gunman was medium height and build. His partner, the third gunman, was chubby with a big, round belly. They were all dressed identically. The guy who had come disguised as the postal worker looked nervous. His eyes were all over the place.

"What y'all want? Money? I ain't bucking. I got money here. Y'all can have it!" my father pleaded.

"Shut up, nigga! You know what we here for. Where

that yay at and that boy, Monster?" the tall gunman asked while calling my father by his street name.

I could tell he was the leader. He had a demanding aura about him.

"What yay? I told you I got money. You can have it."

WHAM!

The tall gunman struck my daddy upside the head, causing him to bend over in pain. Ms. Shay and my sister screamed.

"Daddy!" I yelled and ran over to him.

One of the gunmen placed a gun to my head, and I stopped in my tracks.

Ike Jr. stood petrified with his mouth wide open. He began to wail as his eyes darted between his beloved dying dog and my daddy writhing in pain.

"Shit, man, I told you there is money here. Take it and leave!" my daddy shouted.

"Where the dope at, nigga? I ain't going to ask yo' fuck ass again. I'm just going to start killing shit, and I'm starting with this old bitch right here." He grabbed Ms. Shay. She shrieked in fear.

He then told one of the gunmen to search the house to make sure nobody else was home. Daddy stood up. A trickle of blood cascaded down his shirt. His face showed a painful grimace.

"There's a safe upstairs in my bedroom closet with money in it. Also, there's cash in the top drawer of my desk. There is no dope in this house!" my father sternly said.

I could see his jaw twitching. There would be hell to pay if they let us live.

The tall gunman calmly walked over and aimed his nine-millimeter at Ms. Shay's head as she stood next to me. That was the first time I noticed his black leather gloves.

"Nigga, you think it's a muthafuckin' game!" he yelled, spraying spit.

I could see his lips twisted with malice as the gold grill in his mouth shimmered. He pulled the trigger.

BLOCKA!

Ms. Shay dropped like a sack of potatoes. Her head hit the counter with a loud thump. Blood and brain matter sprayed my face. Keona released a bloodcurdling scream. It felt like I was drowning in a pool of anguish and terror.

Next, the tall gunman grabbed my sister as everyone looked on. The person dressed as the mail carrier started to do a nervous two-step just as the fat gunman who was searching the house ran back into the kitchen at the sound of the gun blast. He had two pillowcases stuffed with money and jewelry. The gunman placed the gun to my sister's head. I gulped for air as I struggled to breathe. I was sinking in despair and suffocating in daunting fear as my heart rate increased.

The tall gunman exclaimed with his gold grill gleaming underneath the ski mask, "I know you got dope, and I know you get heroin, nigga. Don't fuckin' play wit' me, and I know you got that shit stashed." He cocked the gun.

My sister screamed. I felt nauseated, and my legs wobbled. My father threw up both hands.

"Okay! Okay! I can take you to where it's stashed!" my father said.

"Daddy!" I yelled.

The gunman lowered the gun from my sister's head as he shortly glanced at his partner standing next to him as if to say, *I told you so.*

"How far away is it?" the gunman asked. In the background was whimpering and crying.

"Fifty-seven and Martin Luther King Drive," Daddy said as he wiped at the spot where he was hit with the gun upside his head.

"Is the two keys of boy there too?" the gunman asked.

Right then, I knew that someone had set my daddy up to be robbed. Not only that, I was disappointed that he was still in the game after saying that he was no longer dealing with drugs for all those years. I felt a huge amount of disappointment. I couldn't believe Daddy had been lying to me. What the hell happened to keeping it real? I shook my head and frowned at him.

"Yes, it's there," Daddy assured as he cut his eyes at me.

I could sense the anxiousness in the gunman's movements as he looked over at his partners and nodded his head. He grinned underneath his mask. This was what they had come for.

"Just don't hurt no more of my family," Daddy added. The tone in his voice strained like a pensive plea.

"Put his ass in the van," the tall gunman ordered with a snarl as he took out a pair of handcuffs.

They cuffed my daddy and blindfolded him. The whole time, Ike Jr. stared with tears rolling down his face. In my heart and soul, I knew in some warped, crazy way that he was involved in the violent world of Miami's gangland wars.

The guy dressed as the mailman looked out the window and walked over to Daddy, prepared to walk him to the van. He shoved Daddy forward, and he nearly slipped in a pool of blood that gushed from Ms. Shay's dead body and our dog.

Suddenly, Daddy stopped and turned around. The blindfold was a red bandana tied crookedly around his head. I wondered if he could see us when he did the strangest thing and said, "I love y'all. Kadisha, the number is your birthday."

"I love you too, Daddy," we all said in unison.

I didn't have a clue as to what he was talking about. The taller gunman shoved Daddy and gave more orders to the chubby bandit and his medium-built partner. The person disguised as the mail carrier led my father out the door at gunpoint.

"I'm going to take him and get the product. Once I give you a call, you know what to do. I'm going to leave the gasoline can outside the door. Remember what I told you. No witness. No evidence. No problems."

My heart dropped to my gut as my legs nearly buckled. My sister and little brother were so distraught. They didn't know the thugs were planning to kill us. Maybe I was wrong; maybe I was overreacting and panicking. I prayed that was the case.

WE RUSHED OUT of the kitchen, leaving behind massive amounts of blood on the floor. In Daddy's study, the gunman rambled through the desk drawers. They stuffed items into the pillowcases. There was a .45 automatic in a locked drawer. The medium-built gunman tried to open the drawer and couldn't. It was locked.

"What's in here?" he asked in frustration. I could sense agitation and fear as he looked around for something to open it with.

"I don't know what's in there," I lied.

My voice was full of nervousness. The entire time, the chubby gunman was looking at me and my sister with a sneaky expression. I could detect through his mask that he was up to something.

The other gunman took a pair of scissors and pried open the drawer. He found the gun. It was an antique historical object with a pearl handle. It was chrome and platinum. He admired it and aimed it at his chubby partner.

"Man, stop fucking playing before that thing goes off. You remember what happened last time."

"Nigga, that was an accident," he said and tucked the gun in his waistband.

"That's what I'm talkin' 'bout. You accidentally shot me." The chubby guy snorted.

His partner chuckled. I could tell the two weren't playing with a full deck of cards. They were both idiots.

"Where is the safe?" one of the bandits asked.

I realized that he was talking to me.

"It's upstairs in my father's bedroom," I reluctantly responded as my little brother continued to hold back tears. Keona cried softly as her head bobbed back and forth.

"Let's go! Show me where it's at. We ain't got all fucking day," the medium-built person barked.

The entire time, his partner was fascinated by something on the wall. It was the portrait of the naked African queen.

We were marched up the stairs into my father's bedroom. That was his sanctuary. The decor was suited for a king. An assortment of jewelry lined the dresser. There were Rolex watches, diamond rings, and even a gold coin collection that cost a fortune. The thieves began to stuff the items into the pillowcases. They had definitely found a pot of gold. *I knew Daddy had a gun hidden in the bedroom someplace, but where?* I thought as I looked around the room.

Next, the medium-built dude searched through the closet as his partner held us at gunpoint. He shot us an evil look and clocked me in the back of the head with his weapon. My head dropped, and my mouth flew open from the stinging pain that shot through the back of my skull. He hit me for no apparent reason. He was mean as a barrel of snakes, and I couldn't wait for them to hurry up and leave. I said a silent prayer and hoped that God would spare our lives. I didn't want to end up the way Plato and Ms. Shay had.

"Goddamnit! It's locked!" the gunman in the closet scoffed.

I could hear clothes and boxes being thrown about. He then stepped out of the closet. As I watched, my little sister and brother huddled together, crying.

"Call dude and tell him the damn safe is locked," the medium-built thief said.

His partner, the chubby guy, tore his eyes off us and retorted, "Shit, you know how crazy that nigga is. Our order was to wait until he calls us first, and that's what I'm going to do."

"Well, what the fuck we gon' do until he calls?"

The chubby one walked over to his partner. They began to whisper, and I felt eerily uncomfortable.

"Kadisha, what they do to Daddy? They killed Plato and Ms. Shay," Ike Jr. muttered.

I noticed his hands were shaking. His voice was barely audible as he rubbed his red eyes with the back of his hands.

The two gunmen stalked back over to us.

"Y'all bitches take them fuckin' clothes off!" the chubby gunman said, waving the gun at us.

He snatched the envelope full of money from the side of the jeans I wore. His eyes bulged at all the hundred-dollar bills. He quickly stashed the envelope in his pocket before his partner could see it.

I couldn't believe what I was hearing. This couldn't be happening. They wanted us to get naked.

My sister was only twelve; she was just big for her age. She would sometimes steal designer clothes and wear them to school. Boys would try to talk to us both, thinking she was my age.

"My sister is only twelve. What you want us to get naked for?" I blurted out.

I needed to stop them before it started. I needed them to go away and for this to be a bad dream. It wasn't a nightmare that I would wake from. It wasn't. It was real.

The chubby gunman strolled over to me. "Bitch, didn't I tell you to take them fuckin' clothes off?" He slapped me so hard that I stumbled backward.

I staggered, seeing stars. With my vision blurred, I watched my little brother rush him, swinging his fists.

"Leave my sister alone!"

The guy smacked him across the head with the gun. Horrified, I watched my little brother fall on his back, knocked out cold. His little leg began to shake.

"You didn't have to hit him!" I roared.

The chubby one raised his hand to strike me. I flinched and began to take off my clothes. I looked over at Keona on the other side of the room; she was already undressed down to her panties and bra as she cried hysterically. The guy unbuckled his pants, took his penis out, and began to stoke up and down his length. That was when something dawned on me. Big Bee, my father's righthand man, had gone to the store. He said he'd be back soon.

"Hurry up and come back, Big Bee," I prayed.

CHAPTER
Five

Kadisha

He grabbed Keona by the hair and dragged her to the middle of the floor. The man made several derogatory remarks toward her. Keona was swinging at him, trying to make him leave her alone. The man punched her in the stomach and kicked her in the back to get her down. I'll never forget the sound of her crying, begging, and pleading as she called my name to help her.

Apparently, I wasn't moving fast enough for the chubby gunman. He reached for my bra and ripped it off. My breasts hung freely like two hoop earrings as I stood there in my pink panties.

"Dayum dis' lil bitch bad ta' death!" he said with a tone full of lust.

He unzipped his pants and shoved me on the bed. I

closed my eyes and shut them tight. On the bed next to me, I could hear the awful sounds of my little sister crying and screaming as she was violently raped.

My panties were shoved to the side as he tried to find the entrance to my vagina. I heard my sister's assailant grunt and groan. The bed wobbled as he violently penetrated her. I kept my eyes closed the entire time. I tried to block everything out, but I could still hear my sister wailing as she called my name. Time passed. I didn't know how long, but it felt like an eternity. The other side of the bed continued to shake. I could hear his grunting and loud moans as the rhythm of the assailant's pace slowed down. The entire time, the fat, chubby bastard slobbered, kissed, and sucked all over my breasts as he tried with no luck to enter me. I could smell the rank scent of his musty odor, along with some type of liquor.

Finally, he was able to penetrate me, and a sharp shooting pain crept past my walls. My vagina was throbbing. It felt like a bomb exploded inside me. The pain was excruciating! My eyes were shut tight in torment. I opened them and saw my little sister's assailant get up.

He wiped his penis with his shirt and humorously said, "This bitch got blood all over my dick." Then he took out a roll of duct tape and taped her feet, hands, and then her mouth.

My legs were spread wider as my captor plunged inside me so hard. It was so painful as if he found happiness in the pain I was feeling. He seemed to enjoy humiliating me as I cried out in disbelief.

"This bitch got some good ass pussy!" he sang out as he thrusted faster inside me. Sweat dribbled from his stinky body.

His partner stroked himself as he watched and said, "I'ma hit that pussy next, but we got to do something about the DNA. I'll be right back."

He took off out of the room. I heard the door shut, and for a second, I thought about trying dude. Could I wrestle the chubby guy raping me?

I slightly turned my head and saw my sister on the other side of the bed. She was butt naked, and her face was red. A bunch of veins projected from her forehead. Her eyes were bulging wide like they were about to pop out of the sockets.

She was scared as hell.

I had to build up the courage to do something. Should I fight back, shove him, kick, bite, or scratch? The door opened, and I heard footsteps. The other assailant had returned. A dangerous fume hit the air. I quickly realized what it was.

Gasoline! I screamed in my mind.

They intended to burn us alive. "Oh, God, help me. Help! Help me!" I prayed as I was raped.

"Hurry up, nigga. Let me hit that ass before we go. We don't need evidence, and we definitely don't want witnesses. I got the phone call. Everything is a go," the guy returned and said to his chubby partner just as he grunted and shivered.

I could feel his warm semen releasing in my body.

He got off me in a hurry to let his partner take his turn. In that dark moment, sanity had been replaced with insanity. The voice in my head was strong. I was on the verge of losing my mind.

"Get up! Fight back. Do something. They are going to kill you anyway."

The other guy eased between my thighs. I could feel his hard stick throbbing and probing as he squeezed my breasts. He bit my nipple so hard that he drew blood. Ever so calmly, his partner, the chubby guy, walked over to my sister and placed a pillow over her head. This had been their plan. They definitely wanted to hurt us in the worst way.

Blocka!

The muffled shot resonated. Instantly, I felt my sister's body jerk and then stop moving as smoke formed like a halo over the pillow. Horrified, I screamed at the top of my lungs.

At the sound of the gun blast, Ike Jr. woke up. *They are going to kill him too,* I thought as I felt the cold steel of a nine-millimeter pressed to the side of my temple. A pillow was over my face. Death was coming soon. I was doomed. I heard the chamber of the gun cock. Involuntarily, my body went into fight mode. I lashed out and struck my attacker, scratching and clawing. I heard him holler painfully as I raked my fingernails across his face, gouging his eyes. I removed the ski mask and saw his face. The struggle continued as I fought with every fiber and muscle in my body. The gun was on the side of my head as we tussled. Then, a sonic boom explosion rocked my body. I had been shot in the head. Ike Jr. screamed and rushed the attackers. There was another shot fired.

Silence filled the room.

"Nigga, hurry! Let's go!" one gunman shouted.

My body had been doused with gasoline. Semi-conscious, I could vaguely make out what was being said. Perhaps I was dreaming. Perhaps I was dead. There was a bullet wound in my head. I knew because I could feel blood oozing down my neck and merging with the gas.

"Give me your lighter, so I can set this bitch on fire, and we can bounce," the chubby gunmen said, then a voice shrieked in panic.

"Oh, shit! Some big nigga just pulled up in the front yard in a Cadillac Escalade."

"Wait! Wait! Let's wait until he comes into the house and blast his ass, then burn this bitch down and bounce," a voice suggested.

"Okay, let's go!" another voice returned.

I heard footsteps exiting the room. Moments later, I heard a barrage of shots fired. I tried to get up and move, but I couldn't open my eyes.

Seconds later, I heard their footsteps. The attackers had returned. I braced myself for the inevitable. The door abruptly opened.

THROUGH MY HAZE of pain and trauma, I heard a human cry that sounded almost like an animal's. It sounded like a howl of anguish.

Their pain was pungent, palpable. "No! No!" the wailing continued.

Someone was walking around the room, checking the pulse of the bodies, crying like a baby. I felt my body lifted, and my pulse was checked.

A baritone voice melancholically bellowed, "No! No! God, nooo!"

It was then that I realized it was Big Bee crying, howling like a coyote, as he held me in his massive arms. He thought we were all dead. Carnage of bodies was in the room. Somehow, I managed to move my index finger. My lips moved muted, devoid of words. Big Bee took notice.

He wailed, "Kadisha! Kadisha! You're alive!"

I barely opened one eye. It was soaked with blood and the stinging irritation of gasoline. I saw that Big Bee had been shot twice in the shoulder and arm. He was oblivious to his own wounds as he asked me questions, panic-driven on the edge of disorientation.

"Where is Monster? Where your daddy?" He slightly shook my body.

I wish I could have answered, but my lips wouldn't move. He still talked to me as if to comfort me.

"An ambulance is on the way, baby girl. Okay, you gon' be alright. You just keep on breathing. You stay alive. You hear me?" For some reason, he shook me again with his muscled arms. His voice cracked, and I felt his warm tears on my face. "I got one of them, baby girl. I shot his fat ass in the kitchen. You hear me?"

I couldn't answer, but I heard him. Then, from a distance, I heard a siren blaring. The police were coming.

"Baby girl, I gotta move that safe out of the closet. I gotta do it for yo' daddy."

I felt him lift my body and place it back on the bed. At that time, it felt like my soul soared high above the celestial clouds as I drifted off into a comatose state.

CHAPTER Six

Two weeks later

The alarming sound of beeps chimed in my head as I lay in a hospital bed, semi-conscious. I was bandaged like a mummy with all kinds of contraptions hooked up to my body.

A man's voice spoke. "Ma'am, visiting hours are almost over."

"I know, but I am her only family. I have permission. I spoke with her doctor."

"Okay. I'll check," the female voice responded.

I heard a door shut. Someone took my hand and squeezed it. For some reason, that ignited something in my mind. In monothematic flashes, Ms. Shay was on the kitchen floor in a puddle of blood next to our dog, Plato. My daddy was taken out of the house at gunpoint. My sister's

51

eyes watched me as she yelled my name while she was being brutally raped. Then, a gun was to my head during a violent struggle. I fought for my life. A shot was fired.

I flinched and tried to wake up, but I couldn't. My eyes briefly fluttered and closed. I could barely make out my Aunt Esther's wrinkled face. She was my mother's sister. She had papers of some type in her hands. She was ridiculously dressed in what looked like her church clothes, a purple dress with a matching wide-brimmed hat that had dangling rainbow-colored beads.

"You're awake?" she asked and stood over me wide eyed. She then said, "I need you to help me help you and your brother. Sign these papers."

She took my hand and placed a pen in it. I could feel myself signing some type of document. I couldn't acknowledge if I wanted to, but I wouldn't if I could have. I just wanted to help my brother if he was alive. The thing was, Aunt Esther was a two-faced, back-stabbing, double-crossing, gossiping, conniving bitch who had always hated me. She had two daughters, Bernadine and Linda, who were fat and ugly, just like their mama, but all of them had big butts. That seemed to run in our family. All I ever did was fight with my so-called cousins. On holidays, they would come by to eat up all our food. Aunt Esther would complain to Daddy that he was spoiling us too much. Every time they left, a few of our clothes would, too.

I could hear the shuffling of papers as I wondered what she was up to. A door opened, and I listened to the patter of feet. A voice intoned, "Could you please remove these papers off the bed?" The person speaking sounded annoyed.

"Humph," I heard my aunt mutter as she took the papers off my bed that she had scattered.

I realized there was a nurse in the room. She touched my arm to adjust an IV tube and then delicately caressed my face. It was then that I realized there was a tube in my nose that ran down my throat.

"Kadisha, sweetheart, everything is going to be okay. You just hang in there. Okay?"

No answer.

The nurse patted my hand. I heard her feet shuffle as she walked out of the room.

"Bitch!" my aunt hissed.

My mind was in a mental fugue, like I was searching in the darkness, stumbling in a slumber. I couldn't wake up, but I could hear everything.

A door opened again, and for a brief moment, I could hear the cacophony of noises coming from outside in the hallway. The door closed, and footsteps approached my bed. I heard the frivolous shuffling of something strange. I smelled some type of floral scent.

"Hi, Doctor," Aunt Esther said.

"Hello," the doctor responded. Wasting no time, he checked my vitals. He opened my eyes and looked at the pupils with a flashlight.

"Is she going to be okay?" my aunt asked.

"Lucky for her, the bullet only penetrated the right

temporal bone of her skull and exited through the occipital bone, leaving her brain unharmed. The neurologist said her brain activity is normal. The only other concern is the psychological trauma that she experienced. The authorities said she put up a violent fight. The police found one of the attackers' DNA under her fingernails. She's been tested for venereal diseases. All of her tests came back good, and she doesn't have any diseases."

"Yeah, my niece is a fighter," my aunt stated.

The doctor began to remove the gauze from my shaved head. I heard my aunt expel a deep gasp. My shaved head looked grisly. I had over two hundred staples and pins on the right side.

"Oh! Just what in the hell did you do to her head?" Aunt Esther shouted.

"It was a procedure to mend her injuries so that we could stop the bleeding and make sure her brain was not hemorrhaging."

"Uh, uh, that looks like a lawsuit. Y'all done messed up my niece's head!"

"Ma'am, I'm going to have to ask you to leave the room while I tend to my patient."

"Humph!" She huffed indignantly, gathered the papers, and left the room.

Once she was gone, the doctor continued his examination. I felt his fingers walk across my bald skin. The doctor began to talk to me soothingly as if he knew I could hear him.

"You will pull through this. You will be okay. The

swelling will go down in a couple of weeks. You may experience some minor vision problems for a short time. Your balance may be off as well, causing you to have headaches and dizziness."

As he talked, I could feel a cold draft on my head. He started wrapping my head back as he softly whispered, "You'll be okay. You have been through a lot. Continue to keep your faith."

I felt him squeeze my hand. Somewhere in the abyss of darkness, I found the strength to weakly squeeze his hand back and slowly open my eyes. He responded with a gentle smile.

"I knew you could hear me."

A tear slid down my cheek, and he wiped it. Simultaneously, we heard a lot of commotion coming from the hallway. There was a shouting match going on. Suddenly, the door burst open, and all hell broke loose. I heard my girls, Latoya and Shamica, arguing with someone when they entered the room. Then, I heard the voice that I felt like I had not heard in years, my mother. She was also arguing with the nurse, and they were all loud and belligerent.

"You all have to leave. No one but immediate family is allowed in her room," the nurse said.

"I ain't going nowhere. I'm her mama, bitch. Your ass is the one who needs to leave, bitch!"

Aunt Esther cut in. "When did you start being her mama? Make them leave," my aunt sided with the nurse.

The doctor tried his best to calm them down for my

55

sake. He said, "Ladies, please calm down, or I'm going to have security escort you all out of the hospital."

"I want them all outta here," my aunt said.

"We ain't going nowhere!" both Latoya and Shamica said in unison. I could hear the anger in both their voices.

This could've caused a serious problem because my Mom was hood, straight-up ghetto hood. She was born and raised in the Pork and Beans projects. Some wealthy Black folks adopted her sister Esther. Esther was raised differently from Mama. She had never worked a day in her life. She had always had a husband to take care of her. The problem was, a year ago, her fourth husband, James, died. She thought she was secure financially, but instead, she found out her husband was in debt and owed back taxes and creditors. The IRS was currently trying to take her lavish home on a beach in South Miami.

I heard a scuffle. Mama had jumped on my aunt. This was a real problem. Not only was my mom a crack addict but it was rumored that she had AIDS. Her blood could've been lethal.

"Get her off me!" my aunt yelled.

She and Mama could never get along. Aunt Esther couldn't fight a lick. Mama knew that and pummeled her. They stumbled over to my bed, throwing down. Aunt Esther was screaming and yelling. The IV bag attached to my arm nearly toppled over, but the startled doctor grabbed it just in time.

"She's choking me!" Aunt Esther yelled.

A chair turned over. A glass vase full of red roses crashed to the floor. There were more sounds of a struggle, screaming, and shouting.

The doctor told the nurse, "I've had enough. I'm calling security. This is ridiculous."

You know your family is bad and ghetto when security is notified that they need to come to your hospital room.

"Y'all... stop...it!" I croaked dryly with the tube running down my throat. It felt like barbed wire.

Instantly, the commotion stopped. Mama was bent over with her hands on her knees, trying to catch her breath. She looked a hot mess. She had what appeared to be some type of black hat on her head. It could have passed for a trash bag. She was dressed in an oversized sweatshirt and raggedy blue jeans as she held Aunt Esther's awful looking track of hair weave in her hand. My girlfriends both looked at me big-eyed like they had seen Sasquatch.

Latoya finally said, "She's awake! She's awake!"

She and Shamica held hands as they walked up to the bed. Shamica started crying like a baby. That was when the hospital security entered the room. They were two huge white men who looked more like police officers with guns and badges than hospital security.

I heard something metal hit the floor. It was a "stem" crack pipe made from a car antenna. Everyone noticed except the doctor and the security guards. Auntie had a knot on her forehead the size of an egg from where Mama hit her. She looked at my mother like she was thinking about telling, but my mom gritted on her and made a face with a threat that could only lead to another ass whipping. Aunt Esther demurred.

"What is going on in here?" one of the security guards asked with his hand on his gun. For some reason, he stared at my mom.

"Doc, let them stay," I pleaded. My throat hurt so bad when I swallowed; it felt like I was going to die.

The doctor looked between my mother and aunt with pure disdain as he bunched his thin lips up in a tight line across his face. The EKG machine continued to beep in synchronic drones that seemed to resonate in the new silence in the room.

Finally, the doctor said, "You have thirty minutes with her. That's all." He raised his voice for the first time.

As soon as the doctor and hospital security walked out of the room and shut the door, Mama and Aunt Esther were back at it again.

"Stop it! Stop it!" Latoya yelled at them just when my mom had her fist balled tight and was about to slug Aunt Esther again.

"Daddy... Keona... Ike..." I muttered in a maudlin voice, brimming with tears.

Just then, my mother walked over. The entire time, she was giving Aunt Esther the evil eye like it wasn't over yet. She took my hand in hers. Her rough hand was calloused like she had been laying bricks all her life. Her face was ashy. Her volcanic eyes were gaunt, sunken in like she hadn't been to sleep for days.

"Ike Jr. is in the children's ward downstairs. Keona and Ms. Shay didn't make it, baby. I'm sorry." My mother began to sob, and so did everybody in the room except Aunt Esther.

For a fleeting second, I couldn't help but wonder what she was up to as I noticed for the first time that the room was colorful with bright pastel colors. There were flowers and teddy bears everywhere, hundreds of them.

"Daddy?" I asked. That one word took everything out of me.

Fatigued, I began to fall back and stared at the wall. Mama cried harder. Her mouth moved with no words. She buried her face in her hands and sobbed.

Latoya stepped forward; her eyes were bloodshot red and puffy as she held back tears.

"Everything is going to be alright. The funeral was last week. It was beautiful. Everyone says you're a hero because you survived that brutality like a soldier. There was a lot of media there." Shamica nodded her head in agreement. Latoya continued, "They still have not found your daddy yet. I know he is still alive. His friend, Big Bee, is in jail. They charged him with murder and possession of a weapon by a convicted felon. He killed one of the dudes that tried to kill you."

I wanted to open my mouth and say something—to scream, to plead at that point. They needed to know it was

Big Bee who saved my life, but I was too tired to speak. Too tired to even move. I was barely able to turn my head. I wanted to tell her something, but I couldn't. That's when I heard it again. My mother and Aunt Esther were back at it.

"Bitch, gimme dem papers!" my mother shrieked.

There was another scuffle. I looked over to see that my mother had punched Esther in her eye and strong-armed the papers.

"Power of attorney and legal custodian of the house and cars. Executor of all trust funds, bank accounts, and wills. Hell naw, bitch! Is you out yo' fuckin' rabbit ass mind?" my mom yelled.

"Gimme them papers back!" Esther screamed and charged forward.

Mama hit her with a two-piece in her face. The papers went flying in the air. Esther tried to grab my mother. It then occurred to me what Aunt Esther had been up to the entire time. She smelled money, with her being my only close kin. Since my mom was on drugs, she would use my misfortune as a come-up.

Suddenly, the door opened, and two plain-clothed homicide detectives walked in. Both of them were nicely dressed, in their middle to late forties, and African American. One was short with a bald head, a heavyset build, and a big stomach like he had a fetish for donuts. His partner was slightly taller and heavier. He was the cooler of the two. He had on tinted stylish spectacles with slim gold rims. His beard was neatly trimmed. It almost looked like he had sprayed it on.

Both cops surveyed the room. The shorter detective flashed his badge. "I'm Detective Jones from homicide, and this is my partner, Malcolm Steel."

Before he could get the words out of his mouth, Mama, Latoya, and Shamica said their polite hellos and exited the room with the quickness.

Aunt Esther retrieved the fraudulent documents off the floor and said, "She ain't in no condition to talk. Y'all need to let her rest."

"And who are you?" one of the detectives asked.

"I'm her auntie and about to be her legal guardian if I can get down to the notary and get these papers notarized," my aunt said, glancing at her watch and shuffling papers.

She was moving her jaw around like she was checking to see if it was broken. She brushed by one of the detectives, and they exchanged angry expressions as she walked out the door.

I QUICKLY SHUT my eyes and played half-dead. Both homicide detectives walked over to me. I could smell the scent of cologne along with the aura of masculinity as I imagined their eyes looking at me.

I heard the short detective tell his partner, "She's still

comatose. If there is any chance of solving this case and finding her father, we're going to need some type of witness. Time is running out."

His partner responded, "I know. If we can just get some-body to pick Graylin Kelly out of the photo lineup. I have a hunch that will break this case wide open."

Graylin Kelly? My mind churned in a pit of darkness, swirling thoughts like ebb and flow, an endless tidal wave of possibilities. My baby brother was still alive, and possibly my father was too. I had to open my eyes. I had to confront the cops.

"Uhh," I moaned with a slight nod of my head and struggled to open my eyes. But they wouldn't open. The shorter cop nudged his partner just when they were getting ready to walk out the door. They returned.

"Keona... can you hear us?" he asked.

"Yes..." I struggled to speak.

A lone tear slid down my cheek into my ear. The blatant beeps of the EKG machine seemed to drone along, growing louder. Both cops introduced themselves again as if I hadn't heard them the first time. The cop with the gray beard spoke to me so assuringly, so confidently, that there was something parental about him. It pulled me to him, gnawed at me in a way I couldn't understand, couldn't comprehend.

"We gonna find these people that did this to you and your family. I have a little girl in high school. She is my baby. She looks just like you." He took my hand, his voice choked up, and I heard a quaver.

Another tear slid down my cheek. I wanted to wipe it, but my hands wouldn't move.

"We want to show you some pictures. Can you open your eyes?" he asked.

I suddenly got the urge to swallow, to speak. I wanted to regurgitate words, but my throat felt like sandpaper. The strong pain medicine kicked in and made me sleepy. I couldn't find myself, that switch to turn on, to tell my mind to open my eyes.

"Let's go. Leave her alone. The poor girl has been through a lot," his partner said.

But the cop did not let my hand go. In fact, he squeezed it.

I opened my eyes, and they were filled with tears. I began to cry. I couldn't help it.

The detective said again, "Don't cry. We're going to find these people. Can you look at some photos for us?"

I nodded yes as I sniffled back tears. At that moment, I had never felt so alone in my life. The world seemed to be against me as two strangers stood over my bed.

The detective with the gray beard took some photos out of a large brown envelope. "Did you manage to get a look at any of the attackers?"

I gave the cop a subtle shrug as if to say, maybe.

The first five photos he showed me out of the six were unrecognizable. It wasn't until the last photo that I saw a chilling face, a face that I would never forget. The tall attacker had raped my sister and poured gasoline on us. I had pulled his mask off while he was raping me when I put up the struggle before I was shot. Now I had a face with a name, Graylin Kelly.

I shook my head, no, to the cop. I lied. I could see the disappointment etched on both of their faces.

I dozed off to sleep. This time, my sleep was peaceful. I was determined to seek my own revenge and possibly find my father if he was still alive.

CHAPTER
Seven

Kadisha

I was moved from the ICU into a private room with security outside my door 24/7. Even I knew that the toy rent-a-cop security guards that the hospital provided to protect me in case my assailants came to finish the job were no match for the ruthless men who had assaulted and tried to kill me. Besides Daddy, who was still missing, there was only one man whose presence could make me feel safe.

"Where is Big Bee?" I mumbled to my mother.

She had been at my bedside ever since I regained consciousness.

"Huh? What was that?" she asked, getting up from her chair a few feet away and coming closer. She leaned her head down inches from my mouth.

I repeated my question.

"Oh, you're talking about your father's henchman. That big ass muthafucka," she replied.

"Yes, where is he?" My mouth was crusty and dry.

"I think he's in jail," she said.

In jail? Oh my god! I tried to swallow, but my throat felt like sandpaper.

"Mama, I need a drink of water. My mouth feels like cotton."

She poured me a cup of water from a pitcher on the portable table nearby. Then, she held it to my mouth while I took a few tiny sips. I wrinkled my face up. It felt like I was swallowing a brick.

"That's enough," I managed to say, and Mama took the cup away from my mouth.

She had been so caring since the incident. That was in such contrast to how she normally treated me. I couldn't help but be suspicious. In fact, I was suspicious of everyone.

"Someone has to get Big Bee out of jail. He can find Daddy if he's still alive," I groaned.

"Kadisha, I don't want you getting your hopes up about that because, more than likely, your father is somewhere dead in a ditch."

"What did you just say?" I snapped.

"Honey, we have to face reality. Whoever took Ike would know better than to leave him alive. Your father has a reputation. Niggas know he don't fuck around. After what they did, it would be crazy of them not to kill him," she explained.

Her words rang true. Daddy was no joke, and the whole city of Miami knew that he would kill for the slightest betrayal. Harm his family, and it was bound to be a massacre.

Mama was probably right, but I could not accept it. "He is not dead," I disagreed. Hope was all I had left to hold onto.

"Kadisha," Mama said while leaning close to whisper. "Do you know where your father had any money stashed? If so, you should tell me. You can't trust anyone else."

I was appalled that she would ask that question at a time like this. I gritted, "Can't you at least wait until I'm out of the hospital before you go asking me about Daddy's money?" My words came out like daggers, but her insensitivity was her shield.

She waved me off. "Girl, don't nobody have time for your little feelings. If there's money that you know about somewhere, we should move it before somebody else gets to it," she said while looking back and forth over her shoulder for unwanted listeners.

Was she trying to protect me? Or was she trying to get her greedy hands on money that she didn't deserve? I wondered.

I shivered at the next thought that ran through my mind. Could my mother have had something to do with the robbery? She was a crackhead, and crackheads could be so thirsty. I didn't want to believe she was so desperate that she would conspire with someone to have her own children robbed, raped, and killed. *Maybe she was just down with the robbery but didn't expect them to hurt us?*

"I don't know anything about Daddy's business," I blurted. I decided that it was best to keep my cards close to the vest for the time being.

I could tell from Mama's expression that she didn't believe me. She was about to put the press down on me when Steve walked into the room with a bouquet of flowers in one hand and a balloon that read, 'Get Well Soon' in the other. The balloon floated all about as he held on to its string.

"Hey, baby girl, what's up?" He greeted me with a smile as he set the flowers on the nightstand by the bed and tied the balloon to the bed rail.

"Hi." I returned Steve's greeting in a monotone.

Today was the first time he came to visit me in the hospital, and that added to my suspicions.

When he leaned down to kiss my cheek, I turned my head. All he needed was a ski mask, and he would fit perfectly. The same way I recalled one of the robbers looking. *Same height and build*, I said to myself.

"Oh, is it like that? I can't kiss you?" Steve asked.

When he rose, the bottom of his shirt crawled up, and I spotted a gun on his waist. What the fuck was he doing carrying heat? And where the hell was the toy cop who was supposed to be stationed outside my room?

"Don't bother her! She's still weak," Mama snapped.

"And who the fuck are you, anyway?" she demanded with her hand on her hip. Her eyes ran up and down his frame.

Steve introduced himself as my boyfriend. The polite way in which he said it seemed to put Mama at ease. After a while, she excused herself to go down to the cafeteria and get something to eat.

Once we were alone, Steve whispered, "Tell me what happened."

"I don't feel like talking about it," I said.

That was the truth. I had been reliving the horrible events in my head so often that it pounded with a migraine. Discussing it would only make my head hurt worse.

"Okay, but Latoya and Shamika going around telling everybody a whole lot of shit. They're saying that your father's right-hand man set him up," he said.

"That's a lie!" I hissed.

"How do you know? Did you recognize any of the men who ran up in there on y'all?"

"No, and I don't feel up to answering any questions if you don't mind. All I know is that anyone who says that Big Bee had anything to do with what happened is a liar! Big Bee has always been loyal to our family. He would never betray us."

"Never say *never*, Kadisha. Nobody is to be trusted in the game that your father was in."

I curled my lip and gritted. "Not even *you*, I guess."

"Say what?" he replied with a raised brow.

"I'm saying, maybe *you* can't be trusted either, Steve. You had just left my house that day. I've never seen you with a gun until now. Who's to say you weren't involved in this? I mean, you didn't exactly rush to the hospital to check on my condition."

"That's because I was..."

The sound of someone coming into the room interrupted us. I looked up, and Mellow came bobbing through the door. He had a fat dude with dreads tagging along with him.

"Sup, shawty?" He spoke to me while grilling Steve the whole time. "Nigga, what the fuck you doing here?" he confronted him. The soft, fluorescent light in the room bounced off his diamond and platinum grill.

"I should be asking *you* that," retorted Steve. His chest was all puffed out, though their last encounter hadn't gone in his favor.

But he's strapped now, I recalled.

Mellow didn't know that, though. He looked at his man and chuckled. Pointing at Steve, he mockingly said, "This bitch ass nigga done grew some balls."

"I've been had some. What about you?"

Steve's hand was in his waist, and so was Mellow's now.

"Make it do what it do," challenged Mellow.

His boy stepped out of the way. Either he wasn't strapped, or he wasn't an official goon, I concluded as I studied his build.

Quickly returning my attention to what threatened to pop off at the foot of my bed, I cried, "Mellow, please!"

My hoarse cry seemed to have no effect on him; his attention remained focused on Steve.

"Why are y'all bringing all of this craziness up in here?" Tears ran down my face, but their bangers remained on their waist. And thank God *one* of them was able to demonstrate some self-control.

"Kadisha, I'll be back to see you another time," Steve said. "Later for you, fool," he spat back at Mellow before brushing past Mellow's boy and walking out of the room.

As soon as Steve was gone, I frowned at Mellow and hissed, "That was so unnecessary!"

"No, it wasn't," he disputed. "I'm feelin' like that punk ass nigga had something to do with that shit. Let me find out, and I'ma slump that ass."

He bent over and kissed my forehead. "I see you're doing better today." He observed me. Like my mother, Mellow had been at my bedside every day.

He stroked my hair. "Mellow, who is that?" I whispered, gesturing toward his fat friend with a nod of my head.

"Oh, that's my nigga, Clap. He's riding with me until I find the muthafuckas that did this to you and your family."

"Uh... can you tell him to say something? I want to hear his voice." I continued to speak in a whisper.

"Why?" He looked perplexed.

"Please, Mellow. Can you just do it?"

"Okay, shawty, but I don't understand."

He called Clap over to the bed and introduced us.

"How you doing, ma?" Clap asked with a New York

accent that was definitely not anywhere close to the voice of the fat masked man who had violated me. I breathed a sigh of relief.

"I'm fine," I replied.

"Not really, ma, but you're gonna be okay. Just get well. Me and Mellow gonna find these niggas and make them pay for what they did. Your peeps is a legend in these streets. Niggas should have respected that."

I didn't know how to respond, so all I said was, "Thank you."

Clap fell back, and Mellow took a seat in the chair next to the bed. "Why did you need to hear my nigga's voice?" he asked again.

"No reason," I replied, keeping the truth to myself.

Play your hand wisely and keep your cards close to your vest, I warned myself.

CHAPTER Eight

Mellow

"Shawty don't trust me, my nigga. I can see it written all over her face," I said to Clap as we drove away from the hospital.

The sun had gone down, and dark skies enveloped the city. I turned up the Future CD and headed back to the hood.

"Yo', son, don't even trip over that shit. Na mean? Shawty still traumatized," Clap said.

"I feel you, my nigga."

"Damn, fam, you sound like you're about to cry," he kidded.

"Na, neva that. But I *am* fucked up over what happened to her. I still can't believe niggas would get at her father like that. Ol' boy been in the game for years, and his get down is official. They say, back in the day, his clique had the whole city shook."

"Yeah, I heard. Niggas talk about him way up in New York. But dig this. Where is your mind at, homie?"

Clap's accent had switched from New York back to his native Miami tongue. My nigga was born and raised in Pork n Beans projects until he was ten years old. A month after his tenth birthday, his mother got killed, and he moved to New York with an aunt. So, now, he could switch back and forth between both accents and slang.

I glanced over at him in the passenger seat and asked, "What you mean where my mind at?"

"Forget it, my nigga," he said.

"Nigga, say what's on your mind?" I prodded.

"Um, is it still money over everything?"

The question threw me off. My nigga knew I was about gettin' that check, so why was he questioning my get down?

When I pressed him, he said, "Nigga, you know that nigga Ike had millions. Nine times out of ten, whoever snatched him up didn't get it all because muthafuckas like Ike always have a secret stash for a rainy day. You need to play up under Kadisha and find out where that secret stash at."

I abruptly pulled over to the curb and threw the car in park. My hand came up, gripping my Nina, and I placed it to Clap's head. "You must be tired of living, my nigga," I snarled.

He put his hands up and mumbled a lame apology.

I said, "Nigga, you got the game fucked up! I'm not on no slime shit with shawty. I told you, I respected her pops, and I got love for *her*. Don't ever bring nothin' to me about doing her dirty."

I was contemplating whether I should go ahead and put two in Clap's head. Since I had pulled out on him, things might never be the same between us again.

Out of my peripheral vision, I saw a figure creeping up on me from the rear of my whip. It was coming around to the driver's side. My first thought was that it was some fiend who recognized my whip and was about to beg for some dope. In the second it took to formulate my thoughts, I saw an arm raise.

Boc! Boc! Boc! Boc!

Gunshots fired through the side of the door. I ducked and scrambled over Clap out the passenger door. I fell out the door on my hands and knees. When I came up, I was busting back at the muthafucka. Nina was going the fuck off. Blocka! Blocka! Blocka! Blocka!

The bitch nigga sprinted back to his car, hopped in, and backed up the street in reverse.

"Who the fuck was that?" asked Clap, holding a banger that was still cold.

I eyed him like, *Why the fuck you ain't let that mutha-fucka spit?*

I was hot! I dusted myself off and said, "That was that nigga Steve."

He had grown some balls for real.

Two NIGHTS after Steve tried to get at me, I was about to get at a nigga myself. I had heard that this nigga may have had something to do with what happened to baby girl. Whether he did it or didn't, I wasn't sure, but he had more dope than he usually did. That made him guilty in my eyes.

I was riding dolo because after what Clap had let come out of his mouth the other day, I just wasn't feelin' him anymore. We had been tight since elementary school, but that didn't mean shit out in these streets. The nigga had said it out of his own mouth—money over everything. So that included *me,* too.

I guess he couldn't understand why I was willing to ride so hard for Kadisha; she and I hadn't ever fucked around, but I knew she was feelin' my swag. I was feelin' her too, way more than any of the tennis shoe hoes that I fucked with. I hadn't pushed up on her all the way because I hadn't been sure how her father would feel about that. Most street niggas wanted something better for their daughters. Now that tragedy had befallen their whole family, it was gonna take a street nigga to straighten things out and protect Kadisha. I was *that* nigga.

I pulled up on the scene, hopped out of my whip, and went on the porch of an abandoned house to chop it up with my dudes who were out there slangin' work. About five or six of them sat on the stoops, passing blunts back and forth while they waited for fiends to come cop.

"Sup, my people?" I spoke to the group.

They each spoke back.

"Where you been, fam? I ain't seen you in a month of Sundays," my dude Smurf exaggerated as he extended half of a lit blunt to me.

"I been around." I hit the blunt, holding the smoke in my lungs. "This that *real* Kush!" I exclaimed.

"Nigga, we don't blow nothing but this real shit," proclaimed Jay, who was a certified Kush head.

I listened as they continued the conversation they were having before I rolled up. As soon as there was a break in the conversation, I causally steered it toward what interested me.

"Y'all heard about Ike?" I tossed out, finishing off the blunt.

"Yeah, who hasn't?" Smurf answered for them all.

"I heard they hit him for fifteen mil. But you know how the streets blow shit all out of proportion," interjected one of the others.

"Whatever they touched him for, you can bet it was a sweet lick because that nigga been stacking since our asses were in pampers," added a fourth dude, who was known as Carolina.

"I wonder who got at Ike?" I intoned, deliberately making it sound like a casual question.

I knew that if the streets were talking, one of them would repeat what was being said.

Smurf didn't let me down. He volunteered, "They say that nigga, Black, from Opa-locka, had something to do with it. You know he used to pump for Ike."

I damn sure knew that, and it had been said that Black wasn't happy about Ike cutting him off. I knew personally that Black was a grimy-type cat and that he was capable of any type of slimy act imaginable. A few months ago, he had sold me a quarter key of pure remix. I was still waiting for him to honor his promise to straighten me out on it.

"That bum-ass nigga ain't hit no lick like that. He would be around here flossing hard if he had," I said.

"Man, you must not have heard. Black has come the fuck up! He got a brand new 2011 Escalade sittin' on thirty-inch rims, *and* he got Fishscale on deck."

"Shut up!" I replied doubtfully.

"He not lying. That nigga done came up good! And it was just around the time that shit happened to Ike," Jay divulged before walking off to piss on the side of the house.

I listened to a few more of Smurf's reasons for believing that Black had something to do with the robbery until I became convinced that it was a possibility. And even if he had nothing at all to do with it, I owed him a bullet to the head for selling me that bum-ass coke and not making good on his promise to straighten it up.

I'ma get back with y'all later," I suddenly said. I stood up, gave everyone some dap, and then I got in the wind.

Leaving there, I hit up Black.

"Who is this?" he answered his cell phone.

"This is Mellow. Fam, I need you to get at me on what you owe me. I hear you're living good these days, so fuck with me." I offered him a chance to clear the bad business between us.

Black gave me a bunch of excuses for why he couldn't do that.

"Aight, fam, just get at me soon." I hid the anger that I felt inside. *Nigga think this shit right here is sweet.* I bristled at the way he was handling me. *It's all good, though.*

I knew where he laid his head, and I knew where his chick laid hers. So, for the next few days, I watched him, and I plotted. Then, it was time to *get at him* since he wouldn't get at me. And if he *was* involved in the robbery, well, I was gonna serve him for that, too.

It was dark outside when I parked at the end of the street and got out. I was rockin' a black and gray Oakland Raiders fitted pulled low on my brow. I walked with a purpose as I passed by a fiend or two shuffling out on the block.

I spotted Black twenty yards away, posted up on the hood of his whip, parlaying with a redbone chick who looked like she had ass for days in her faded skinny jeans. I slipped Nina out of my waist and held her down by my side as I approached from the opposite side of the street.

I had shot several niggas before that night, but I had never killed. My heart was thumping; an adrenaline rush hurried my steps. I kept my head tucked down as I closed the distance between Black and myself.

The girl was standing between his knees with her back to me. She was admiring his chain when I put Nina to the back of her head. "Don't turn around, and I won't hurt you." My tone indicated that I was not to be tried.

I removed the banger from her head and pointed it at Black. "Make one country move, homeboy, and I'ma push your shit back! Do you understand me?"

"Yeah," he replied with fear in his eyes.

"Let me see your hands, nigga," I growled, and his hands immediately rose above his head.

"Okay, shawty, lay on the ground on your stomach. Don't look back at me, or I'ma kill you. Do you understand?" I spoke at the back of the chick's neck.

"Yes, I promise I'm not going to look at you. Please just don't hurt me." Her voice trembled with fear as she proceeded to do as I commanded.

When she was face-down on the pavement, I lifted the fitted a few inches over my brows so Black could see my face. The recognition was instant, and then the question in his eyes came out of his mouth.

"What's this all about, my nigga? I told you I'm gonna straighten you out," he cried.

"This ain't just about that. This about Ike too," I snarled.

He recognized the name, of course, because Ike had been his connect. I tried to read his expression for signs of guilt, but it was blank. So, I served him street justice, which was the same as in a court of law. *Guilty until proven innocent.*

I squeezed the trigger and heard Nina echo, and then Black's whole face splattered. I grabbed him by the shirt and pulled him off the hood of the car where his body had slouched. His head fell to the side, and his face was a mass of bloody tissue and bones when I pulled it close to mine.

"This is for Kadisha," I said, real low.

Blocka! Blocka!

I let go of his shirt and watched his corpse slide to the ground.

Next to Black, shawty was screaming. She jumped up and dashed off. I aimed Nina at her back, but I did not squeeze the trigger. There was no need to; she had not seen my face. I pulled the fitted back down low over my brow and trotted back to my whip.

CHAPTER Nine

Kadisha

Steve didn't visit me again until the day before I was released from the hospital. We had it out real good because I felt that he hadn't really been by my side since the incident. For someone who was supposed to be my boyfriend, he had let me down tremendously, I told him.

"I'm just staying in my lane, Kadisha," he claimed.

"What exactly does that mean, Steve?" I eyed him with growing discomfort.

"I'm just saying... you don't need me here. You have plenty of visitors, and I'm not just talking about family and friends. You think I want to roll up in here and see Mellow all up in your room like you're his woman? Me and that nigga got beef, yet you welcome him into your space like everything is all good. But, quiet as it's been kept, I think that nigga may have something to do with what happened."

The accusation hit me like a ton of bricks. Mellow had been so sweet and caring since the incident. Could he really be that conniving to come visit me every day, pretending to be concerned, when really, he had caused all of this? My heart said no, but I didn't know who to trust.

I looked at Steve real hard. He was wearing a new platinum chain that looked very expensive. Could *he* have had something to do with the robbery? Had he used some of the money that he took from Daddy to purchase that chain? Maybe he was pointing the finger at Mellow to hide his own guilt.

I had overheard Daddy say one time, "Be careful of the dog that brings you the bone." This made me look at Steve through squinted eyes.

I fluffed a pillow up behind me and sat up in bed, leaning back against the headboard while studying Steve like I would study a science experiment. "How do you know that Mellow had something to do with what happened?" I questioned.

He ran a hand down his face and nervously chewed on the inside of his mouth. "I didn't say I know it for a fact, but something is not right with that nigga," he beat around the bush.

"Don't tell me what you think. Tell me what you *know*. Because right now, everybody is pointing the finger at a different person," I said with frustration in my voice.

I let out an exasperated sigh.

"It figures you don't wanna hear nothing against that nigga, 'cause you're all on his dick lately. I'ma fall back and let you have him if that's what you want. But mark my words, Kadisha, when the truth comes out, that nigga's hands are gonna have your people's blood on them."

He turned to walk out of the room.

"Maybe yours will, too," I hurled at his back.

That stopped him in his tracks. He turned around and stalked back over to the bed.

"What the fuck did you just say?" he asked.

I could see veins pop up on the side of his head, and his mouth was twisted in a scowl.

"You heard me. I said maybe when the truth comes out, *your* hands will have blood on them, too."

He grabbed my face and brought it close to his. Pain shot up to the top of my head because I was still swollen and sore. "Aww! You're hurting me!" I cried.

"No, Kadisha, you're *hurting* me!" contested Steve. "I would never be down with anything like what was done to you and your family. I'm not that type of dude. You should know that. But I'ma charge that one to the heart because I know your mind isn't right. Time will show you who you can trust." He pressed his lips to mine and said, "I love you." Then he left without looking back.

I buried my head in the pillow and cried. Tears of confusion poured from my eyes, and I sobbed from the enormity of what I was going through.

No matter how I thought about it, I just did not know who I should trust. All I knew was that Keona was dead. Ike Jr, I had been told, was in a coma due to swelling in his brain. Daddy's body still had not been found, and Big Bee was still in jail.

The only thing I was sure of was the name and face of one of the men who had taken my loved ones from me. His face haunted me in my sleep. It haunted me every hour I was awake. At first, the fear that face provoked would cause my body to tremble. Soon, the blood in me that was my daddy's turned that fear into anger, then turned that anger into a thirst for vengeance. Of course, as it stood, I could not present as a formidable match against the ferocious killers who had perpetrated this crime against my family. I had been nothing but a sheltered teenager up to that point, but I was determined to become as cold and ruthless as those I sought vengeance against.

A chorus of voices neared my room, and seconds later, my mother, my aunt, and Latoya came through the door.

"Hi, baby. I see you're awake. We were down on the pediatrics floor, sitting with your brother," Mama said. Worry lines creased her forehead, and it resembled a paper sack that had been uncrumpled.

"How is he doing?" I asked, choking up.

"Not very well, I'm afraid," Aunt Esther answered for my mother, who was biting her lip, trying to sniffle back tears.

"I want to see him," I said.

No one responded, which indicated that his condition was so bad that they thought it would be best that I not see him. *Okay, I will go see him on my own.*

"Your only concern should be getting well," advised my auntie.

"Sure. But am I *not* supposed to be concerned about my brother?"

"Of course you are, Kadisha," she replied. Then, she changed the subject to what they had eaten in the cafeteria for lunch.

Mama rolled her eyes at the ceiling. I looked away from her and Aunt Esther to my girls.

Latoya beamed, "Good afternoon, bestie. You look good today."

"You sure do," Shamika chimed in.

I didn't have to look in a mirror to know that was a lie. I *had* to look a hot mess.

They fussed over me for an hour or more. Perhaps their compassion and concern were genuine, but I viewed it with skepticism. Especially Mama's. Not a day had passed without her asking if I knew where Daddy had left a stash.

"Now, Kadisha, don't try to play me like I'm dumb. I'm sure you know where your father's money is hidden," Mama had repeatedly said to me under her breath. No matter how many times I denied it, she wouldn't back off.

I lay there, trying to make one plus one equal two, while the others talked amongst themselves. Their chatter aggravated me. I was in no mood for it. Auntie and Mama bickered over whose house I would stay at when I was released from the hospital. I had not decided on that myself, but I did not like either option. I fell asleep, pondering my choices.

When I awoke, the room was silent and absent of visitors. I sat up, rubbed the sleep from my eyes, and scanned the room for the night nurse. I was grateful that she was nowhere around because she acted more like a prison warden than a caregiver.

I let down the guardrail and swung my legs over the side of the bed. Then, I picked up a pair of paper booties off the nightstand and slipped them on my feet. When I stood up, I felt dizzy. I took a drink of water from the plastic cup on the portable table nearby. That made me feel better. Bracing myself for my journey, I wrapped my hand around the portable IV and wheeled it alongside me as I crept out into the hallway.

"Well, hello? What are you doing up and about in the middle of the night?" asked the security guard stationed outside my door. He was a fat, older gentleman with a gray afro and a fatherly voice.

I smiled at him politely. "Shh! I'm going down to the pediatrics ICU to see my little brother."

"I'm not sure you're supposed to be up on your feet. Let me go get you a wheelchair, and I'll whisk you down there and back before anyone can miss you," he offered conspiratorially.

A minute later, he was pushing me down the hall toward the elevators in a wheelchair. I tapped my foot nervously as we watched out for the night nurse and waited for the elevator to stop on our floor.

Relief washed over me when the elevator finally arrived, and the security guy hurried me inside. I said, "Thank you, sir."

"No thanks needed, young lady. I was about to doze off just sitting there doing nothing," he confessed.

I smiled my understanding.

Watching the numbers above the door as the elevator descended down to the pediatrics floor, I got a queasy feeling in my stomach. I didn't know what to expect when I saw Ike Jr. I tried to prepare myself for the worst, but no amount of emotional preparation could insulate me from the way I felt when I saw my little brother in the children's ICU.

The nice security guy wheeled me right up to my little brother's bed, and then he left the room to allow me some privacy.

I looked at the different tubes running from Ike Jr's mouth, nose, arms, and chest into nearby machines. The tears instantly fell. He was curled up into himself, almost in the fetal position. He looked so fragile and helpless, but he had been so brave that night.

I opened my mouth to say something encouraging to him, but what came out was a loud sob. "Oh God! Oh God!" I cried.

I reached up and took his small hand in mine. "I love

you, bruh bruh. I love you so much. You tried to protect us..."

I could say no more. My emotions overwhelmed me. My shoulders heaved up and down as I fought in vain to hold back the tidal wave of tears that spilled from my eyes like rain pouring from an overburdened cloud.

Visions of that night crept up on me in such a horrible clarity that my whole body shuddered. I squeezed my eyes tight, hoping to force the images out of my mind, but they were as deeply embedded as crime is among the impoverished.

When I snapped my eyes open, the present was no better; Ike Jr. was comatose, but he was a little hero in my eyes. *I'm going to get them for what they did to us,* I solemnly vowed.

The next morning, the usual suspects were in my room, trying to convince me that I should come and live with them as opposed to going to stay with anyone else. Mama and my auntie almost came to blows about it. After last night, I had no energy to intervene; I just listened and shook my head in exasperation.

Mellow came through the door. He stopped in his tracks and looked at me questioningly as if to ask, *Am I walking into a family quarrel?*

I waved him on in.

"Don't pay them any attention," I said as he pulled a chair up to the side of my bed and asked how I was doing in the midst of all the fuss.

"I'm feeling very sad," I admitted, staring at his platinum and diamond grill for some reason.

"What's wrong, shawty?" His tone revealed genuine concern.

"I went down to pediatrics to see my little brother last night, and he is in such bad shape." Tears rimmed my eyes.

"You did *what?*" Mama cut in, abruptly ending her quarrel with Aunt Esther. "You're not supposed to be out of bed." She was acting as if she couldn't understand that I wanted to see Ike Jr.—damn my medical condition!

"See, that is the reason you must come home with *me* when you're released tomorrow. You need someone who'll look after you and make sure you're not up walking around until you're well," she insisted.

"Hmmph! You need someone to look after *you*, to make sure you don't relapse for the twenty-millionth time," Auntie pointed out.

Mama glared at her like a prizefighter does his opponent before the opening bell.

"Will you two please not start?" I begged them, covering my ears with both hands.

"Fine! I'm going back home," Mama said. She could be so dang theatrical at times.

She turned and stormed out.

"Now, Auntie, you know that was not a nice thing for you to say," I chastised.

"I'll go and soothe her hurt feelings."

Auntie hurried out to catch Mama.

Mellow looked like he wanted to laugh, shake his head... do something to express his feelings over what he had just witnessed.

"Excuse my family. They're just a little dysfunctional," I quipped, allowing a smile to wash onto my face.

He looked at me, staring deep into my eyes... sort of like he was trying to peer into my soul. "Kadisha, who do you want to stay with?" he asked. Not once did his eyes leave mine.

I took a minute to consider the question before replying, "To be honest, I don't want to stay with either of them." I frowned because I had no other options.

I could see the wheels spinning in Mellow's mind, and I correctly guessed what he was going to offer before the words came out of his mouth. "No, Mellow. I don't even know you like that." I quickly declined the invitation, though he had yet to extend it.

"Damn, shawty, at least consider it. I mean, you'll be safe with me. That's the number one priority right now. And you'll have your own room. So, it's not like I'ma be pressing you for sex."

"I don't know, Mellow. On one hand, it sounds like the better option, but—"

"Just think about it." He cut me off.

By the time morning rolled around, I had decided to throw all caution to the wind and take Mellow up on his offer to move in with him temporarily. When I announced that to Mama and Aunt Esther, they roared their disapproval and threatened to have me committed to a mental institution.

Like I said, Mama could become a drama queen in the blink of an eye. But at the end of the day, I ignored their threats and followed my own mind for better or worse.

CHAPTER Ten

Mellow

"I'ma take good care of you, shawty," I promised Kadisha as I carried her into the bedroom and gently laid her on the bed.

"I told you I could've walked," she said, sounding a bit embarrassed.

"Nah, baby girl. I got you. I'ma take care of you and nurse you back to health. In the meantime, ain't nobody gon' come up in here and fuck with you. If they do, I got something for their asses."

I walked to the closet and brought out my choppa and Mac 11. I walked back over and sat on the bed with both weapons next to me.

"What type of guns are those?" asked Kadisha.

"This is an AK-47." I pointed to the choppa.

"And this is a Mac 11 submachine gun. And I got more heat in case those aren't enough." I took Nina off my waist and placed her on the nightstand.

Kadisha grew quiet. I wondered if seeing those weapons was causing her to have flashbacks.

"You okay, baby girl?"

"I'm fine," she muttered.

"You damn sure are. As long as you're here with me, can't nobody harm you," I tried to reassure.

She managed a faint smile. It brightened her face even though it was still swollen and bruised, and there was discoloration underneath both eyes. There were only light traces of blood soaked through the heavy gauze bandages wrapped around her head.

When she realized that I was staring at her, she turned her face away from me.

"I know I look horrible," she said as she began to sniffle.

I wrapped my arms around her and told her that she was still as beautiful as ever to me. "Your bruises will eventually fade away, and your scars will heal. Don't worry about any of that, baby, just concentrate on getting well. Okay?"

She cried in my arms for a few minutes. Each time she sobbed, it squeezed my heart as if her pain were my own.

"Why are you doing so much for me, Mellow?" she asked.

I didn't have to contemplate the question. The answer came without hesitation. "Kadisha, I used to watch you every time you were in my presence. It didn't matter how many other girls were around. You stood out in the crowd. I always felt that you would be mine one day. I just couldn't see what you saw in that nigga Steve."

"He was okay, I guess. But you still haven't explained why you're doing so much for me. I mean, we hardly know one another," she delved deeper.

All I could do was keep it one hunnid with her about how I felt. "You're right. We don't really know each other like that, but I can tell that you're way more than the average young chick out here. For one, you come from boss pedigree. That alone makes you stand out because I truly believe that the apple doesn't fall far from the tree."

Kadisha studied me intensely as if she was trying to gauge the sincerity of what I said. Her gaze didn't bother me because there was no game in my words. I told her, "From here on out, it's over between you and Steve. You hear me?"

She nodded yes.

"If that's a problem, tell me now," I demanded.

She shook her head no.

"Good," I said. "Because I'm about to lay it all on the line for you."

I tried to read her heart before continuing. "The other night, I killed this nigga named Black. I slumped him because I heard that he might've had something to do with the robbery at your house. Whether or not those rumors were true don't matter. His name came up, so I got at his ass. And that's what I'ma do to every muthafucka whose name gets connected to what happened."

Kadisha didn't say anything for a long while. When she finally spoke, all she said was, "I'm going to rest now. I feel so tired."

"Okay, shawty, get some rest. I'ma step out for a while. I have to go make a few moves."

"No! Please don't leave me here alone," she cried, springing up and wrapping her arms around me. She was squeezing me so tight I could hardly breathe, and I could feel her trembling.

"It's okay, Kadisha. No one knows you're here." My crib was in the Grove, and no one knew where I rested my head.

Kadisha held me tighter.

"When I leave, put the deadbolts on the door and don't answer it for no one." I gently removed her hands from around my back, then reached into my pocket and handed her one of my two cell phones. I took out the other one and called the phone in her hand.

"Lock that number in. It's the number I'll call you from if I need to speak to you. If you need me for anything or if you hear a sound, don't hesitate to call me."

My words seemed to do little to relieve her fear of being left alone. It flashed in her eyes like a neon sign. I understood her anxiety. She had gone through a traumatic incident that had probably scarred her forever. I hadn't had the heart to ask her to tell me what happened that night. Any details that I knew had either come from what was being said in the streets or what Kadisha's big-mouthed friends were running around spreading. Those two hoes were gonna make somebody shut them up.

"Do you have to go?" Kadisha whined.

"Yeah, shawty, I gotta go make a few moves. And while I'm out, I'ma see if the streets are saying anything new about what happened."

"I don't want you to go." She grabbed my shirt and wouldn't let go.

I bent down, kissed her forehead, and then removed Nina from my waist and held it out to her. "Here. Do you know how to use it?"

She just stared at the nine.

"Okay, shawty, I know your head is all fucked up right now, and I can understand why. But I'ma need you to toughen up just a little more. You come from the bloodline of one of the most legendary gangstas to ever walk the streets of Miami." I left the rest unsaid.

Kadisha bravely reached out and accepted Nina. "Be careful. It's loaded, but the safety is on," I said as I sat back and carefully took the gun out of her hands.

"Let me show you how to handle it."

"My daddy used to take Keona and me to the shooting range and target practice. I kinda remember how to handle a gun, but just show me anyway."

I removed the clip and the round that I kept in the chamber.

For the next thirty minutes, I showed her how to hold

the gun when firing and how to engage and disengage the safety.

"Do you feel safer now?" I asked after she caught on.

"Yes, I do," she mumbled.

"Good. Now, I'm about to leave. Come lock the door behind me."

At the door, I kissed shawty goodbye, then hit the streets to handle my business.

CHAPTER Eleven

Kadisha

As soon as I closed the door behind Mellow and slid the deadbolts in place, I went rambling through the apartment. I was looking for anything that was taken from our house the night of the robbery. I rifled through drawers and closets, looking for items of clothing that matched those of the robbers.

Steve's warning that Mellow may have been involved in the robbery could not be overlooked, regardless of how unlikely it seemed to me. With Daddy missing and Big Bee in jail, I was lost. Mellow was stepping up to the plate for me in a big way, and he was doing a good job of winning my heart. But if I was going to give it to him, I had to eliminate every suspicion that he had been involved in the robbery of my home, the killing of Keona, and the disappearance of my father.

In the closet of the spare bedroom, I found several shoe-boxes full of money wrapped in assorted colored rubber bands. I searched my memory to recall if I had ever seen any of Daddy's money wrapped in the same colored rubber bands. I had not, but that proved little because Daddy never allowed us to see much.

When I went through the dirty clothes in the bathroom, I came upon black clothing with dried bloodstains on it!

Shocked and terrified, I dropped the pants and T-shirt on the floor and started hyperventilating. Could this be the blood of my sister or brother or Ms. Shay?

No. I was absolutely certain that Mellow had not been one of the men who ran up into our house. I had seen the face of one of them, and I would've recognized Mellow's voice had he been one of the others. Besides, he was not built like either of the two whose faces I had not seen that night.

That didn't mean he hadn't set it all up or that he hadn't been waiting wherever Daddy had been taken to. I didn't know what to think. And that was the reason I had feigned inexperience about guns when Mellow gave me his 9mm to keep for protection while he was away. Daddy had shown me how to handle a weapon very well.

Hours later, when Mellow returned home, I was sitting on the bed with the bloodstained clothes at my feet.

"How you feelin', shawty?" he asked, coming into the

room with a backpack slung over his shoulder. The expression on my face must've answered his question.

"What's going on, Kadisha?" he asked, tossing the backpack on the floor next to the soiled clothing at my feet. I could tell by the look on his face that he recognized the clothing and the inference I was making.

"No, Mellow, *you* need to be telling me what the fuck is going on!" I had the nine gripped with both hands, pointed at his stomach.

He didn't even flinch.

"Before you shoot me with my own gun, do you mind telling me why you've been rambling through my shit? I mean, this is the thanks I get?" he questioned with a look of hurt on his face.

"Whose blood is that on your clothes, Mellow?"

Now, the implication hit him square in the face. The look on his face changed from one of hurt to anger in the bat of an eye. "Fa real, shawty? Are you muthafuckin' fa real? You think that's your people's blood on those clothes? You judge me to be a grimy nigga like that?"

"You haven't answered my question." I tightened my grip on the strap.

Mellow shook his head in utter disbelief. "Kadisha, I'm feelin' some kinda way right now," he said.

"So am I," I spat back.

"Yeah. I feel you, but don't let your mind play tricks on you. Remember what I told you earlier today about a nigga named Black?"

"I remember," I muttered.

"Well, that's whose blood is on my clothes. I meant to burn 'em. Now, will you put that gun down before you fuck around and accidentally pull the trigger?"

I lowered the gun and then allowed Mellow to take it from my hands. As soon as he did, I started sobbing. My shoulders heaved up and down as I let it all out. Mellow sat on the bed and took me into his arms. "It's okay to cry, baby girl," he comforted.

He held me against his shirt. It was soaked with my tears.

"This is the last time I'm going to cry," I promised Mellow and myself. "Will you please bring me some tissue?" I asked.

He got up and went to the bathroom, returning with a wad of tissue. I blew my nose until my head hurt. "I apologize for going through your things. If you want me to leave, I will," I offered.

"Nah, we good," he assured me and then sealed it with a quick kiss.

"I really am sorry," I said again.

"It's all good, shawty. Let's forget all about that." He bent down and picked the backpack up off the floor. Dumping its contents out on the bed, he announced, "When you feel up to it, I'll take you shopping for clothes. I kinda figured that you might not want to go back to the house to get your things."

Money was all over the bed.

"Thanks, but I'm going back home to get some of my things. I know it's going to be tough on me to go back there, but it's something that I have to do," I explained.

I dreaded making that trip, but I was determined to overcome my fear. "Mellow," I called his name softly while he counted his money.

"Yeah, baby. What's up?"

"If I ask you to do something, will you say yes?"

"Depends on what it is."

"No, you have to say yes regardless."

"Aight. I'll say yes."

"Thank you."

"Well, what do you want to ask me?"

I swallowed back my nervousness, and then I said, "I want you to teach me to kill."

CHAPTER
Twelve

Mellow

"Teach you how to kill, huh? I heard that, shawty." I laughed. She could not be serious.

"I'm not joking, Mellow. I want to learn how to kill with no remorse. The same way those men did when they came to my house."

"But you're nothing like those men, Kadisha. I could teach you how to kill a muthafucka, but no one can teach you how *not* to have feelings about it once you kill them."

"Did you feel anything after you killed Black?" she wanted to know.

Her question caught me off guard, and I had to think about it for a minute.

My first instinct was to act hard as fuck; pretend that I

had slumped the nigga, and never even gave it a second thought afterward, but I was too real to fake it to her.

"I'ma tell you some real shit. Black was the first nigga I put in the ground. The night I killed him, he was sitting on the hood of his car, and this red chick was standing between his legs. I crept right up on them. I made the girl lie face down on the ground, and then I grabbed Black by the collar, shoved my gun in his face, and pulled the trigger. The nigga's head jerked back from the impact of the bullet, and blood was all over his face. I snatched him up by the collar again and pulled him real close so that his face was only inches from mine. He was so close; I could see the bullet hole in his cheek."

I saw that Kadisha was listening closely, unbothered by the gory details. So, I continued. When I was done telling her in full detail about the second shots that I popped in Black's head and how his blood sprayed all over me, I admitted, "I had no remorse for slumping that maggot, but I have dreamed about it a few times since."

"What if he had nothing to do with it? That would mean you killed him for no reason. Would that bother you?" she probed.

"Not at all." And I meant that. Shit happens. "You know what, shawty? The gun that you were gonna shoot me with, that's the same gun I used to kill Black."

"And?"

"Oh, it don't bother you that you held it?"

"No, but it bothers me that you still have it. Aren't you supposed to get rid of it?" she naively asked.

"Hell nah. They only do that shit in the movies. Niggas in the streets have a dozen bodies on the same gun."

Kadisha shook her head.

"That's careless, isn't it?" she asked.

I just hunched my shoulders, like, oh well.

She went to take a bath while I finished counting the money on the bed. When she emerged from the bathroom, she was wearing one of my T-shirts. It fit her like a long nightgown, and it was raised up in the back because she had an ass as plump as a beach ball.

"Are you hungry?" I asked.

"No, I don't have an appetite." She sat on the bed with one leg folded under her and the other dangling over the side of the bed.

Her luscious thighs promised pleasure like none I had known before. I averted my eyes away from all that temptation because it was way too soon after the incident to approach her about sex.

"What were you staring at?" she asked.

"Nothin'."

"Liar." We both laughed.

Moments later, the laugh lines at the corners of my mouth were turned upside down. I listened to Kadisha describe the home invasion. She fought valiantly to hold back tears but lost the battle when she described how her sister and the housekeeper were killed. She even wept while describing the shooting of their dog.

The entire time she was telling her story, I was wondering how a man of her father's stature could slip so badly like that. When muthafuckas ran up in your spot, it usually meant that someone close to you had set it up. Because the average nigga in your circle didn't know where you rested.

"Will you take me to visit Big Bee?" Kadisha asked after she had told me everything that happened that night.

She dried her tears with the backs of her hands and waited for my answer.

I pondered the question for a minute or two. Something told me that Big Bee wasn't as loyal as she believed, but I kept that to myself and agreed to drive her to the jail to visit him.

CHAPTER Thirteen

Big Bee

Somebody fucked up bad. That's all I kept telling myself as I lay on top of my bunk in the Dade County Jail. There was no way to pinpoint the mistake until I knew who the culprits were. Ike had been in the game a long time, and he had plenty of enemies. He had moved far away from the hood to avoid the very thing that had happened.

Ike and I went back to his Boobie Boy days. His children were like my own. I won't ever forget what some lowdown muthafuckas did to Keona and Ms. Shay. They tried to do the same to Kadisha and Ike Jr., but luckily, they survived. I always knew Kadisha was a fighter. I could see that in her, even though Ike spoiled her rotten, as he did the other two.

Something about Kadisha was different from the other two, though. She was an A student in school, but I could tell that she had a mind like her father's, a mind tailor-made for running a street empire.

Speaking of her father, my mind went back and forth on whether I believed he was still alive. Most times, I felt that he had to be dead because only a fool would allow him to live after what was done to his family.

Nah, he's most definitely dead, I accepted. *But I'ma avenge him with all I got when I get out of here.* That's what I was thinking when I heard my name called for visitation. I hurried and got myself together, and then I alerted the guard that I was ready.

When I took a seat behind the thick Plexiglas, Kadisha was seated on the other side of it. Her face was bruised and puffy. I stared at her with tears in my eyes. Somebody had to pay!

"Hi, Big Bee," she said into the phone.

"Hey, there. I'm glad to see you. Are you okay?" I asked, concerned.

"No, not really. Big Bee, do you know who those men were that came up in our house?" She got straight to the point.

"No, but I intend to find out. And I'm going to find out what happened to your father."

"Do you think he's still alive?" Kadisha asked with hope-fulness in her voice.

I couldn't bear to extinguish that hope because it looked as if she needed it in order to go on. "Let's hope so," I said.

"He's still alive," she said with so much conviction that I almost found myself believing it, too.

Changing the subject because our time was getting short, I lowered my voice and whispered, "Kadisha, you have to move the safe."

She looked at me curiously through the glass.

"The safe that was in the closet, I put it in the trunk of your car before the ambulance, and the police showed up that night. Is your car still in the yard?"

"I'm not sure. How did you get a key to the trunk of my car?" she asked with a puzzled expression.

"I was with your father when he purchased the car, and it came with a spare set of keys. I had the spare set because I'm the one who drove the car from the dealership, and I forgot to give it back to your father," I explained.

I cut off any questions that Kadisha had; time was of the essence. "Move the safe," I sternly instructed.

"Okay, I will," she promised.

"Did your father ever give you the combination?" I asked because I was sure she would need the contents inside the safe. And if Ike had told anyone the combination, it would be her.

"No. Daddy never told me those kinds of things."

"Maybe he has, but you didn't know it. Think hard. Has he ever given you a set of numbers that you had no idea what they were for?" I urged her to try to recall, but she drew a blank.

"It's okay, just go move the safe... asap," I reiterated.

"Oh, the keys are buried under the dirt, inside the large flowerpot in the backyard."

"Okay."

We talked for fifteen more minutes that passed by like seconds. Then, my time was up. Before I was escorted back to my cell, I asked, "Where are you staying?"

"With a friend," she replied.

"What's this friend's name?"

"Mellow," she revealed.

The name sounded very familiar, but I could not place it with a face. I strained my mind to remember where I had heard the name before. It didn't hit me until I was being led away by a guard.

When the name registered, I whirled around and shouted to Kadisha. "You can't trust him. He's the enemy!"

But Kadisha was gone.

CHAPTER
Fourteen

Kadisha

My visit with Big Bee left me with more questions than answers. Most of all, I wanted to know what was inside the safe. But how would I get it open without having the combination? I wondered. I could not recall Daddy giving it to me. *Oh, well, I need to go get it ASAP, like Big Bee urged me. I'll worry about the rest after I do that,* I decided.

Mellow was parked at the curb waiting for me when I came out. I was glad because I felt self-conscious about the scarf that I wore around my head, and the bruises on my face were still very visible. I had noticed Big Bee staring at me in shock at my appearance, though he had tried not to let his reaction show on his face. I certainly didn't want anyone else to see me like that.

"How did the visit go?" Mellow asked as soon as I was in the car.

"It was okay," I replied. I strapped on my seatbelt and turned the music down a few decibels. "Can you take me by my house?" I asked.

"Yeah, that ain't a problem, shawty." He drove off without questioning me about it.

We talked about inconsequential things during the drive out to my house. My nerves became more rattled the closer we got to my street. I knew that seeing the house would bring back memories of what happened, but I had to endure that.

As we turned onto my street, all the houses in the plush neighborhood that had felt so familiar to me just weeks ago now felt like the homes of strangers as we passed them by. Even in daylight, the street looked eerie.

I knew that no matter what the future held, I would never feel safe in that plush residential neighborhood again. It may as well have been a cemetery.

As we drove down to my house, my eyes searched for one thing. I spotted my BMW parked right where I had last seen it. It was in the driveway next to Daddy's SUV, which was the red Mercedes and the metallic gray Navigator. But there was also a strange car parked behind mine.

"Mellow, I think someone is inside," I said, frightened. "I've never seen that car before." I pointed.

"Aight. Stay in the car. Maddafact, get behind the

wheel. If anybody comes out without me, you mash out," he instructed.

"I'm scared."

"Don't be. Just do as I said." He reached under his seat and handed me the 9mm. "If any funny style shit jumps off before you have time to back out of the driveway and get ghost, let this bitch pop off."

With that said, he slid out of the car and approached the house with apprehension. He held a second gun at his side; it was a huge military .45. The blue steel gleamed in the ardent sunlight.

My heart pounded in my chest like a bass drum as I watched his every stride. Just that fast, my hand began to tremble as I held the 9mm in my sweaty palm and whispered a silent prayer.

I scooted behind the wheel and waited for what felt like an eternity after Mellow entered the house. As I looked at the unfamiliar car parked in my yard, I couldn't help pondering once again, whose car was that? And why were they there? Had the killers returned, and what were they looking for? Me? The safe? A tremulous shiver came over my body. I was terrified. Mellow was in the house with the possible assailant, and God forbid there was more than one person inside. My mind churned as riveting thoughts gnawed at my conscience.

"Hurry, Mellow! Hurry!" I said aloud in a pensive plea, nerves on edge.

Suddenly, gunshots rang out from the house, shattering the quietness of a second ago. I stifled a scream as I shook uncontrollably. The gun was in my right hand as I watched the door and waited for Mellow to come out, but he didn't. I wanted to go inside after him, but I couldn't. I was paralyzed by fear.

Something very terrifying dawned on me. What if whoever it was inside doing the shooting came out and saw me?

That caused me to panic even more. Then, I remembered something that Mellow said. He told me to leave if anything popped off.

"Fuck! Fuck!" I banged my hand on the steering wheel.

I was full of anguish and despair. How could I just drive off and leave Mellow in the house? I looked over and saw a glint of shimmering sunlight cast off the door handle as the front door slowly opened....

My breath lodged in my throat. I couldn't breathe; fitful anxiety completely consumed me. Then, a face appeared with gaunt eyes and hollow cheeks. The person looked almost demonic as he glowered at me. It wasn't Mellow. Fear shot through my body.

I needed to go!

As I struggled to turn the key in the ignition, the key nearly fell from my hand. The guy at the door lurched forward and down the front steps. At first, I was certain he was going to chase after me. Instinctively, I leveled the gun, prepared to squeeze. Then, I saw Mellow step out from behind the guy.

I breathed a huge sigh of relief. Mellow had a tight grip around the man's shirt collar as he shoved him down the front steps, striking him violently upside the head.

The guy howled in pain as he almost fell to his knees. His face would have struck the ground if it hadn't been for the tight grip Mellow had on the back of his shirt collar.

Seeing that Mellow had control of the man, my hands stopped shaking, and my breathing slowed a bit.

As they approached, I noticed the guy's shirt was covered in blood. It appeared that he had been shot several times and was leaking badly. I distinctly heard him babbling, begging, and pleading for his life.

Mellow viciously struck him again and again. Droplets of blood splattered on the windshield, causing me to cringe. I will never forget the deadly scowl that was etched on Mellow's face. This was his gangsta... crude and indomitable.

"Kadisha, pop the trunk! Pop the fuckin' trunk!" he yelled at me.

Frantically, I searched for the button underneath the dashboard. I was all thumbs as I fumbled around. The entire time, Mellow continued to viciously pistol whip dude.

"Fuck nigga, who else had something to do wit' it?"

"Man, I told you, Black nem," cried ol' boy.

WHACK!

Mellow struck him again, opening a big gash on his fore-head. A shower of blood spewed out of the new wound. I had to turn my head, or else I was going to be sick to my stomach.

"Nigga, you gon' tell me everything I want to know when I'm finished with yo' bitch ass!" Mellow threatened.

Just then, I found the latch to the trunk. It opened with a thump.

"Get yo' fuck ass in da trunk, nigga!" Mellow barked.

"Man, you gon' kill me. I'ma bleed to death in there," he complained.

"Nigga, you gon' bleed to death out here if you don't get yo' bitch ass in that trunk! I'ma bust another cap in yo' ass!"

WHACK!

The guy continued to plead, but his pleas fell on deaf ears. Mellow managed to push him into the spacious trunk. I heard it slam shut. Mellow was moving fast and with precision like it wasn't his first time abducting a dude in broad daylight, shooting him, and loading him into the back of a car trunk.

He hopped into the driver's seat. His clothes reeked of the foul scent of blood and something else I couldn't describe.

"Who is that guy?" I asked in a high-pitched tone, a falsetto of fear.

"That nigga part of Black's crew. I was right. Black did have something to do with it. I'ma take him to the spot and make his bitch ass talk," Mellow gritted, causing the diamond grill in his mouth to sparkle menacingly. There was a speckle of what appeared to be blood on his chin as he turned the ignition.

Suddenly, I remembered something I had forgotten in all the chaos.

"Hold up! Wait!" I shrieked, grabbing Mellow's arm. "I have to check on something."

"Wha-da-fuck!" He grimaced at me.

The perplexed expression on his face said, *Have you lost your damn mind?* His chivalry was gone, replaced by a ruthless thuggishness.

He stared at me with a quiet but quizzical expression.

A loud *boom* broke through the silence. The guy in the trunk began to pound on something inside. Mellow turned and snarled over his shoulder, "Nigga I'ma come back there and slump yo' fuck ass if you make one more sound."

Silence.

He then focused his attention back on me. His eyebrows were knotted in a tight line across his forehead as if his anger was brewing like a tempestuous storm. Or maybe it was his urgency. We needed to leave!

"Mellow, can I trust you?" I said, barely above a whisper. I could feel my bottom lip trembling.

Mellow looked at me with piercing eyes that searched mine for an answer. I didn't keep him waiting a minute longer. I explained to him the real reason I wanted to come to the house. Mellow understood, and he agreed to help with the mission.

We found the keys to the BMW exactly where Big Bee said he had stashed them. Together, we hurried to the back of the car. I slid the key into the trunk, and a terrible thought crossed my mind. What if Mellow shot me in the back of the head as soon as he saw the safe?

I was buggin'.

I held my breath as the trunk popped open, revealing the steel safe. It gleamed in the luminous sunlight.

"Goddamn!" Mellow droned behind me.

I exhaled a weary sigh. I didn't have the combination, but at least I had found the safe. God only knew what was inside it.

"That bitch looks heavy as shit, shawty. Do you think you can drive this car?" he asked.

I shrugged. "I don't know. But if I *have* to, I will." I was shaking all over, and he must have noticed it.

"Fuck!" Mellow muttered and stalked off, leaving me to stare after him.

I watched with apprehension and dread as he got into his Chevy, put the car in reverse, and backed up next to the BMW. He popped his trunk and hopped back out with that big ass .45 leveled as his pants sagged low.

"What are you doing?" My voice screeched as a fuchsia-colored dusk started to descend on the sky.

"I'm finna move the safe into my whip. You're in no condition to drive," he said and opened the trunk.

The guy inside was writhing in agony as he lay in a pool of blood. I couldn't help but fear the worst. The guy was in bad condition, and the trunk would become his casket.

"Are you serious?"

"Hell yeah! Your pops may have a couple mill in that safe," Mellow speculated. Then added, "Besides, I can get two bodies in this bitch. The safe will fit easily."

With my help, he was able to hoist the safe out of my car. It teetered on the back fender of Mellow's whip as he strained with it.

I could see corrugated veins protruding out from his face and neck. His brawny muscles flexed and coiled as he struggled with it, and then he let it drop on dude's leg in the truck. I heard the bone snap, and his leg turned all the way in the wrong direction under the weight of the steel safe. The guy screamed in pain.

WHAM!

With the quickness, Mellow punched him in the face. "Fuck nigga, I'm not gon' tell you again to shut the fuck up!"

The guy began to groan and whimper in excruciating pain, with his lips pressed tightly together. For some reason, I stared at his leg twisted in the wrong direction. I had never seen death beckoning—up close and personal—but this appeared to be it.

I realized this was Mellow's prologue to torture, and it was impressionable. It would forever be indelibly imbibed in my young mind. Warily, I glanced over at Mellow. He must have read my thoughts. He twisted his lips with disdain as the diamond in his mouth sparkled.

"Dis nigga is a wrap! He gonna tell me everything I wanna know and some mo' shit when I get finished wit' his punk ass." He slammed the trunk so hard it made me flinch.

It suddenly occurred to me that Mellow's intention of making dude talk was going to be nothing short of murder. I wanted to be there to question the guy. That was *if* I could tolerate all the gory blood.

I needed to toughen up.

"Mellow, I want to be there when you question him," I said in a small voice.

I was a bundle of emotions. I didn't even realize the nine was still lying on the bumper where I had placed it. I picked it up.

Mellow stared into my eyes, obviously trying to read my sincerity. With a raised brow, he asked, "Are you sure, Kadisha? Because it's gon' be ugly. I'm telling you right now!"

I gave him a confident nod. Then, I answered unwaveringly. "Yes, I want to be right there."

It was on!

As we pulled out of the driveway of a place that was once dear to me—the plush palatial confines of what used to be my happy home with my family—sadly, it only reminded me of the tragedy. The deaths, shattered dreams, and stolen tomorrows. It all seemed to flash back in my mind. I couldn't help it; I choked back a sob. My eyes welled with tears. I was all alone.

Mellow made a right down Biscayne Boulevard and glanced over at me. He saw that I was about to break down again.

"Come on now, don't do that. Don't cry. I got you. Please believe me." His voice cooed and nestled in a place that harbored so much hurt in my soul. All I could do was sniffle back my tears and lower my eyes.

We stopped at a red light. Mellow reached over, took my hand, and leaned forward. He kissed me tenderly and held me in his arms.

I offered no resistance. It felt good. I needed his touch, his kiss. For him to hold me in a strong embrace. I melted in his arms.

Right then, right there, at that moment... at *that* time, on a desolate street, if he had asked me to, I would have given him my everything, including my goodies. Dude had been going hard for me, way beyond the ordinary call of duty for a thug.

He affectionately caressed my shoulders and said, in a gentle whisper, "Think about your pops. You gotta be strong..."

A car horn blared loudly behind us. The light had turned green. We looked at each other, embarrassed. The guy in the trunk had started beating hard on the inside of the hood again. Mellow pulled away from me.

I thought of something. It hit me like an epiphany. When the gunmen were leading my dad out of the kitchen as they were abducting him, he had said to me, "Kadisha, the number is your birthday."

What number? Could he have been talking about the combination to the safe? Yes, it had to be! Daddy always shared his secrets with me, especially during a crisis.

"I think I got it!" I blurted.

"Got what?" Mellow asked as we passed by a strip club called the Rolex.

"The number to the safe."

"I sure as fuck hope so 'cause that bitch gon' be hard as fuck to open," he said and took my hand.

I leaned over and rested my head on his shoulder. That's when we both heard an unwelcome sound at the same time.

CHIRP! CHIRP! It was the sound of the beast. I looked in the rearview mirror. A police cruiser was pulling us over.

"Fuck!" Mellow scoffed as he reached under the seat for the big .45.

"What are you about to do?" I cried.

"Listen, shawty, a nigga can't go back to the joint. This burner alone will get me sentenced to an L. Only God knows what's in the safe. I'd rather have trial on the street. I want you to get out of the car and start walking."

"No, no." I resisted his demand. This could not be happening! *Lord, tell me this is a sick dream.*

Just that fast, things had suddenly worsened. Mellow was fully intent on having a trial in the street. He tightened his grip on his burner, and the knot in my stomach doubled me over.

"Oh, my god! Oh, my god!" I cried and braced myself for the unthinkable.

CHAPTER
Fifteen

Kadisha

The cop got out of his patrol car with caution as cars passed at the busy intersection. He had his hand on his holster as he approached, staring at the trunk of the car. He wore mirrored wraparound shades, a white shirt, and beige Dickey pants instead of a police uniform. His badge hung around his neck, dangling on a string. He appeared to be in very good physical condition like he worked out at a gym.

"Get out and dip, shawty," Mellow said as the cop approached. He eased the gun from under his thigh. I didn't move; I just sat rigid with fear.

"Can I see your license and registration along with proof of insurance?" the cop asked.

"Officer, what's the problem?" Mellow asked. Then he cut his eyes at me, signaling for me to go.

"Your right taillight is malfunctioning."

Bam! Bam! Bam!

The guy in the truck was beating on something. The cop cocked his head to the side as if listening. Mellow eased his hand onto his strap.

"It's just a different color cause one of the bulbs is brighter than the other," Mellow said.

"Get out the car, start walking," Mellow whispered again.

My heart was pounding so fast in my chest that it felt like I was going to faint.

"Did you say something?" the cop asked and bent down to look at me.

With my face bandaged and disfigured, he did a double take. He did a horrible job of hiding his shock at my appearance.

Bam! Bam!

"And your name is?" the cop asked and looked back at the trunk as several cars sped past.

The cop inched closer, out of oncoming traffic. The entire time, Mellow had never reached for his license or registration. That's when it dawned on me. He had no intention of showing it to the cop.

"M... my... my name is Kadisha Spencer." For some reason, my voice was high-pitched.

"Kadisha Spencer?" the cop said with a raised brow, just

as a Mack truck sped by, stirring hot air. The cop walked around the car to my side.

"Get out! Get out!" Mellow whispered under his breath in a hushed tone as he shifted in his seat uncomfortably. Just that fast, he'd broken out in a sweat.

The cop squatted at my side of the car, looking at me. He had a mocha-colored complexion, like he was mixed with some other ethnicity, maybe Spanish. He had a mane of curly hair, starting to recede at the top, giving him the appearance of a much older man, but his face looked vaguely familiar. It wasn't until he removed his sunglasses that I realized I knew him from somewhere.

"You look much better now since the last time I saw you," the cop said with a smile.

Confused, I asked, "Do I know you from somewhere?"

Mellow expelled a deep sigh and glared at me, a warning to shut up and let the cop go.

"I'm Sergeant Malcolm Steel over Miami Dade's homicide division. I visited you a while back and showed you a photo lineup. You may not remember me." He squinted from the sun.

"Ohhhh, yes, I remember you," I genuinely said.

I was so nervous that my right leg was shaking. He was one of the cops who showed me the picture of Graylin Kelly, the guy who raped and killed my sister and shot my baby brother in the chest. I was heavily medicated that day, but everything suddenly rushed back to me.

"Normally, I wouldn't even be out this early, especially

driving a squad car, but the Commissioner, along with the Chief of Police, organized a special task force to work on this case. This really hit home for a lot of people, including myself. You deserve a beautiful prom night like any other teenager. I promise you, we will get the culprits. So far, we have come up with a DNA match to one of the suspects," he said, causing my heart to swell with joy. He continued, "It was from the suspect that was murdered, unfortunately."

"Oh," I said, suddenly unenthused.

I had hoped he was talking about the other guy who had gotten away. All I could do was give him a somber nod. I glanced in Mellow's direction as he continued to stare at me and the cop with a menacing scowl as perspiration glistened off his chin and forehead. He wanted our conversation to end.

"Do you think you can look at the photo lineup again? We really need your help," the cop said.

I nodded and shielded my eyes from the sun as I pretended to wince in pain. "Right now, I'm on my way home. I need my pain medication," I said.

The cop touched my arm. "You're a strong girl, and you have been through a lot. Here is my card. Call me in a day or two to make an appointment to stop by the station, or I'll pay you a visit," he said and passed me his card.

"You two be safe and get that taillight fixed," the sergeant said, peeking in at Mellow.

"Yes, sir!" Mellow responded as sweat poured off his forehead.

Just as the cop got ready to walk away, the guy in the trunk began to beat again.

BAM! BAM! BAM!

The cop stopped and listened, looking down at the trunk, just as a yellow school bus full of loud, rambunctious children, screaming and hollering, stopped and let out some kids.

BAM! BAM! BAM!

"Help!!" the guy began to yell from inside the trunk.

Mellow turned up his stereo, blasting 2 Chainz. The cop frowned and turned all the way around like he was trying to figure out where the screaming was coming from. Then he glanced at the yellow bus.

Mellow drove off as I checked the rearview mirror. The cop was walking back toward Mellow's car with his hand cuffed under his chin.

"Muthufucka! Punk ass nigga in the trunk still beatin' and shit. That was too close," Mellow angrily said, then wiped the sweat from his brow with a deep sigh.

"You're driving around with a bad taillight?" I asked, making a face at him.

"It works. It's a different color than the other one, but it's legit. He just wanted to fuck wit a nigga. If you hadn't been in the whip, I woulda had to wet his ass up."

"Dude in the trunk had me so scared," I said with my hand over my heart.

"That nigga almost fucked us up. I got somethin' for his ass." Mellow sneered, checking his rearview mirror.

The diamond iced-out grill in his mouth sparkled sinisterly. For some reason, I found myself staring at him and all the tats covering his muscular body as I wondered once again if I could trust him. I thought about Graylin Kelly, one of the dudes who had done those terrible things to me and my family. At any cost, I was determined to find him. He knew where my father was.

"Damn, shawty, what you looking at a nigga like that for?" Mellow asked as he grabbed my hand and squeezed it.

I felt an electric surge go through my body and turned my head to face the bright sun. The Miami heat was sweltering, and the bandage on my head was uncomfortable. We stopped at a light on 25th Street. Mellow turned down the music. The beating had stopped coming from the trunk, and I could tell his mind was elsewhere. I needed to talk to him. As far as I knew, he was the only person I could trust.

"A dude named Graylin Kelly was one of the dudes who raped and murdered my sister and shot my baby brother," I said with a quiver in my voice.

Mellow pulled his hand away from me like it had been burned as he looked at me with a shocked expression. His eyes squinted into tiny slits, then he banged his hand on the dashboard, making me flinch.

"Come on, Kadisha, why you gon' say some shit like that?" He frowned at me.

"'Cause the police showed me a photo lineup with his picture in it. That was the guy who did the home invasion.

He raped my sister. Shot her in the head." I choked back a sob, telling myself I was not going to cry again.

"Did you tell the cops that?" For some reason, Mellow was fuming mad.

"No! My daddy didn't raise me to be a snitch. I'ma get his ass myself."

"I thought you said they had ski masks on," he responded as he turned the corner.

We were on the same block he lived on. I detected a certain paranoia about him as he drove up to the old house that he rented. It was in the cut, in a wooded area, on a grove. There was an orchard of orange trees, palm trees, and lots of shrubs and bushes.

"Because I fought him when he tried to rape me, too. I pulled his mask off. I saw his face and scratched him." Then, something occurred to me. I raised my voice in a pungent plea. "Why you act like you don't believe me?" I screamed at him, losing my temper.

Mellow expelled a deep sigh. He suddenly looked uncomfortable. We pulled into his dirt driveway. There were several whips parked in the yard under a shade palm tree. One of them was a new black Dodge Charger, sitting on 24-inch rims. Next to it was a white 350 Mercedes Benz.

"Because G is my cousin," he finally said.

His entire demeanor changed, and so did mine. He parked the car and turned the engine off. There was a soft, balmy breeze in the wind. I was completely at a loss for words; I didn't know what to say or do.

Bam! Bam! Bam!

The guy in the trunk was back to making noise.

"G?" I repeated, looking at him in disbelief.

"Yeah, Graylin Kelly. G is his street name. We're cousins." For some reason, after Mellow said it, he slumped down in his seat, staring out into the distance.

"Your cousin?" Inadvertently, I slid away from him.

Instantly, I regretted telling him anything I knew about the incident with my family. My daddy always told me that blood was thicker than water.

"Maybe you're wrong! Them folks have been at my cousin, G, for a minute. You can't trust them crackas."

"I'm not wrong! I'm telling you what I saw with my own eyes. He was on top of me, raping me. He put a gun to my head. I fought and scratched his face... he... he... shot... me." I began to cry. Just talking about it made me feel like I was reliving the horrific experience all over again.

Mellow glanced over at me. "Don't cry. I'll check G out... Okay?"

He placed his hand on my shoulder, and I pulled away from him.

"Take me back home. I'm not feeling you right now," I honestly said.

He pulled me close and wrapped his arms around me. "Please don't go, Kadisha. I'm sorry... it's just that G is my cousin. His moms is my aunt. He's four years older than me, and he taught me a lot of this street shit. He caught his first body when he was fifteen. Him and his crew, the John Doe

Boys, are notorious. They're suspected of being involved with over a hundred bodies and shootings in Liberty City, their turf. I would have to really be on my A game to even step to him, but I will. I promise."

I had heard of the John Doe Boys and seen the killings all over the news. They were a ruthless gang, caught up in a vicious drug war in Miami. I also knew they were beefing with a guy named Rah-Rah because my girl, Shamika, had given him some. She said he stayed strapped, even in bed.

"So, you don't believe me?" I asked.

I looked up into his handsome face as I wiped the tears in my eyes. He kissed my forehead. It felt good to be in his arms.

"No, it's just that I don't want to believe you. But in my heart, I know it's a possibility that it could be true. I know what G is capable of doing. Home invasion is one of their specialties. I am not going to turn on you. If it's him, I'm going to deal wit' him, too," Mellow said, still holding me in his arms.

"Kadisha, you have to trust me. I'ma fuck wit'cha. I like you a lot. I always wanted you from the first time I saw you in school. I won't betray your trust. You have to believe me, okay?"

He wiped the tears from my cheeks, causing me to turn and glance into his brown eyes. I saw sincerity and a dude who cared about me. I just prayed I wasn't wrong.

"Come on, I'ma make this nigga talk. Then we gotta lug this heavy ass safe into the house."

CHAPTER Sixteen

Kadisha

A horrible smell hit me in the face when Mellow opened the trunk of the car. I almost fainted. The guy was still lying on his back with the safe on his leg. His leg was twisted all the way around in the wrong direction, contorted in a horrible position. I had never seen so much blood in my life. The rancid scent made me want to vomit.

"Come on, man, lemme go," the guy pleaded as a bubble of blood rose and burst from his nose.

WHAM!

Mellow struck him upside the head with the butt of his gun. A trickle of blood ran down his face.

"Fuck nigga, I thought I told your bitch ass to be quiet. Beatin' on the fuckin' trunk n' shit," Mellow said.

"Man, you gon' lemme die in here." The dude started

crying, blathering, begging for his life. A grown man turned into a baby.

"I ain't going to kill you. That's on ery'thang I love, as long as you tell me what I want to know," Mellow said and turned to me, giving a sly wink.

WE WRESTLED with the safe for nearly twenty minutes before we were able to get it out of the car and onto a blanket. Next, Mellow made the dude climb out of the trunk and crawl on the ground into the house at gunpoint. The guy was in such terrible condition that he left a trail of blood behind him. Strangely, I felt no sympathy whatsoever for him.

Mellow tied him to a metal folding chair with an electrical cord. The entire time, the guy whined and complained, thrashing about, as blood continued to ooze from the gaping holes in his chest and face. Mellow continued to reassure him that he wouldn't kill him if he told us what we wanted to know.

There was a 72-inch TV on the wall. I caught a reflection of myself as I stood with my arms folded over my chest. The bandage on my head looked like a turban. My face was still slightly swollen and bruised. I tore my eyes away from my reflection just as Mellow took out his chrome-plated

9mm and began to menacingly pace around the dude. The guy watched Mellow with his one good eye.

"First question, and if you lie to me, I'm going to push your wig back with my nine. No more beatings. It's a bullet to your dome from here on out, na'mean?"

The guy nodded his head. His chest heaved, and it seemed that he was having trouble breathing and about to go into shock.

"What's your name, nigga? And where you from?" Mellow stopped pacing and asked.

"Michael Thompson... I'm from Liberty City..." The guy writhed in pain as he looked between me and Mellow.

Mellow gave me a knowing glance like he was onto something. We both knew that my ex-boyfriend, Steve, was from Liberty City and so was G.

"Who set the lick up for you to go into the house?" Mellow calmly asked with the gun at his side.

"Man, I didn't have nuttin' ta do with the home invasion and killings—" he began to rumble.

With the quickness, Mellow cocked and raised the gun to the guy's head.

"Fuck nigga, dat ain't what I asked you. Who sent you to the house?" Mellow placed his face inches away from the guy's, yelling and spraying him with spittle.

"B... Black n'em sent me days ago... but when he got murdered... I still came anyway."

"You said Black n'em. Who else was involved?" Mellow asked.

The guy was visibly shaking. His bloody lips moved, but no words came out at first. It was as if he was taking his last breaths. Then, he finally said it.

"Steve and G... They wanted me to go in there to find a safe," he said, barely audible, and then hung his head as he struggled to breathe.

My knees nearly buckled as Mellow turned and looked me square in the eye. I thought I saw what looked like murderous rage. Whatever he was feeling contaminated me; it was as if I was becoming someone else. All the death and bloodshed was having an effect on me. I was becoming immune to it. All I could think about was revenge as I looked at dude strapped to the chair. For the first time in my life, I wanted to murder someone—him.

"Where is my father?" I raised my voice. It hinted at tears, but it wasn't sad tears. More like vengeful tears.

"I... I don't know where your father is. I swear to God..."

I walked over. I could hear Mellow muttering something to himself; he had a look of disgust on his face. It was apparent that I was telling the truth. His cousin, G, was responsible for all the violence, death, and destruction that had ruined my life.

"Here, you said you wanted me to teach you how to kill. Kill 'em!" Mellow dared me. Without a shadow of a doubt, I was up to the challenge.

"No! No! I told you everything you wanted. You said you wasn't going to kill me." The guy began to weep harder as he thrashed in the chair. He tried to scoot his chair away from me.

"I didn't lie to you. I'm not going to kill you. She is." Mellow nodded for me to finish dude.

My palm was sweaty, and my hand shook with an insurgence of power. The kind that comes from when your entire family has been tortured and murdered. I thought of my little brother lying in the hospital, barely clinging to life. I was the only one to seek revenge. There was no doubt whatsoever that I was going to pull the trigger. He represented everything that I'd lost, everything that I had once held dear to me—my life, my love, my family.

I placed the gun to his head, next to a gash that was already spewing blood. "Where is my fuckin' daddy? Where is he? Tell me! Tell me!" I bit my bottom lip so hard that I nearly drew blood as tears started to streak down my cheeks. The barrel of the gun was pressed to his head. Mellow looked on with a raised brow and a malicious scowl on his handsome face.

"I swear to god! You gotta believe me—"

My hands were shaking...

I squeezed the trigger.

BLOKA!!

The gun jerked in my hands. His neck snapped back as blood sprayed my clothes. The barrel of the gun smoldered with a ribbon of smoke. Mellow's lips formed an incredulous O as he looked at dude with a gaping hole in his head. Dude sat perfectly still with his one good eye open. I had never killed anyone in my life; I didn't know it could feel so good.

It's the best feeling in the world to avenge my family's death, I thought as I held the chrome-plated nine.

"Muthufucka!" Mellow cursed.

At first, I thought he was talking about me, but then I realized his mind was elsewhere.

"Steven and G..." he mused.

Then he walked over to the table and picked up one of the blunts that were lined up next to a scale with some powder on it. He fired it up and plopped down on the couch next to the safe.

"I got Steve. Can you take care of your cousin G?" I said confidently, still holding the smoldering gun.

Mellow gave me a befuddled stare as he shrugged. "You stay out of this. Besides, I dunno... it's gonna be hard. G is my first cousin. He raised me, took me under his wing when I was a shawty. G is a beast with gunplay. Plus, wherever they go, they roll deep with them choppers. And with Steve, he's a coward. But if he's down with G, that is where he suddenly got heart from. His punk ass took a few shots at me the other day. Now, his back is against the wall. He'll kill you if he thinks you know he was involved in your father's abduction."

"Then that's a chance I have to take!" I said with confidence. For some reason, I was still staring at the dead dude; the 9mm felt good in my hands.

"I don't want you to take that chance. You don't understand, these niggas is killers, official goons, at least G is. Steve is just a fuck boy follower, but if he's rolling with G, then like it or not, that makes him a force to be reckoned with. As for my cousin G, he and his crew stay strapped and on constant alert mode 'cause they beefing with every-body, especially with Rah-Rah and them Overtown niggas. I gotta be careful and think things out," Mellow said and passed me the blunt as his eyes shifted between the heavy safe and the dead dude. Then he did the strangest thing. He looked down at my thighs as if he was in heavy thought.

I declined the blunt. I had never smoked weed in my life, but all my homegirls were weed heads.

"Gurl, you betta puff on this bitch. You say you wanna be a part of this life. To catch a gangsta, to kill a gangsta, you gotta think like a gangsta, na'mean?" he said, causing his diamond grill to sparkle and shimmer ominously.

I once again found myself mesmerized by his bedroom eyes and fine ass sculptured body, covered with tattoos. There was one tattoo in particular that caught my attention. It was a beautiful picture of a baby in a casket enveloped by heavenly wings with the letters, RIP.

Hesitantly, I looked between the tattoo and the blunt, then back over to the dead dude as I slowly reached for the blunt. I took my first hit of weed, Purple Kush, and coughed like I was going to lose a lung. Then, instantly, the euphoric, tranquil high soothed my mind and took me into deep thought, murderous thoughts, to a place I had never been before as Mellow's words resonated in my head. *"To catch a gangsta, to kill a gangsta, you have to think like a gangsta."*

I was a gangsta's daughter, born and raised in Miami's notorious Pork and Beans Projects all my life. I had been exposed to gunplay, drugs, and murder ever since I was an infant. I knew more than the average street nigga. It was just that I was smart, had a high IQ, and graduated from high school at the head of my class. I should have been entering college, but from that day forward, I would never be the same.

As my mind plotted and conspired, I suddenly realized I was still holding the gun. Blunt in one hand, gun in the other. As Mellow looked, I felt a surge of energy, like a bitch who was about to seek revenge. I kissed the gun and saw my murky reflection on the television as I imagined the havoc I was going to wreak on my unsuspecting enemies. At seventeen years old, my rite of passage into that life was a body and a blunt. My sacrifice would be my life. Mellow may not have known it, but he had just helped create a bad bitch with an insatiable desire for mayhem, murder, and revenge. Nothing or no one was going to stop me.

Not even him.

"So, what happened to all the dope and money my father had left on the streets?" I asked Mellow.

For some reason, the weed had me in deep thought, contemplating my next move. Like I was the reincarnation of my dad... like a gangsta's daughter.

Mellow just looked at me for a minute like he was

surprised I would ask such a question. Then he said, "Shit, them niggas gon' try to cuff it if don't nobody step to them."

"Well, I'ma do that."

"Do what?"

"Step to them niggas about my father's money, just as he would have."

"You trippin'. Your dad's lieutenant is Buckey Brown. They holding down the Pork and Beans projects. I can tell you right now, they ain't paying you, and them some scandalous ass fuck niggas. You gon' have to charge that to the game."

"Charge shit! I know Buckey Brown and all them. You got to member. I grew up in the projects."

Mellow just gave me a blank stare. I knew what he was thinking. Bucky Brown and his crew that ran the projects were like a mission impossible for Mellow because project niggas were the worst niggas. It was impossible to penetrate the concrete and steel fortress if you weren't from that project. What looked like unorganized mass confusion was reasoned, organized, and designed to cause confusion and chaos, but I was born and raised there.

"Them niggas gon' give up my daddy's paper and product or else—"

"Else what, Kadisha? You're starting to think like a dude," Mellow complained.

"What's wrong with that?" I shot back.

"You're not! You're a chick!" Mellow made a face.

"My daddy told me a bullet will make a nigga humble," I

confidently said because there was no doubt in my mind what my dad would have done in that situation.

I had stayed up too many nights listening to my dad plot on his enemies as he and Big Bee used my bedroom for their headquarters. There were times I played sleep and times my daddy didn't care whether I was asleep or not. It was as if he had prepared me for this very moment.

CHAPTER Seventeen

Kadisha

L ater that night, I sat in the living room, faded, with a dead body reeking of blood and heavy thoughts on my mind. Mellow beat on the heavy steel safe, trying to get it open with a sledgehammer, then a blow torch. He was making enough racket to wake the dead dude. I could only imagine what was in the safe—money, drugs, guns. Maybe there was a clue as to where my father was.

Mellow's phone continued to ring, and each time, he would stop what he was doing and glance at the number, then reluctantly look at me.

"Gone answer it," I said. All the while, I knew it was one of his little hoes. *I'll have to take care of the problem with his whorish ways,* I thought.

He ignored my sarcasm about his bitches calling. Flustered from not being able to get the safe open, he sat on the couch next to me and wiped the sweat from his forehead. His muscles flexed and coiled. I just happened to glance over, admiring his fine ass physique, and again, I wondered about the tattoo.

"Damn, shawty, why you staring at a nigga like dat for? That weed got you quiet as shit, plotting." He smirked at me and squeezed my inner thigh. Then he looked back over at the safe with a scowl. He was really aggravated that he couldn't get the safe open.

I gave him a shy smile and rolled my shoulders as I tried not to look at his nice body. I thought for a second, and then reality hit me again, and I felt sad.

"It's just so much going on. My baby brother is still in the hospital in a coma. Big Bee is in jail charged with murder—"

"Fuck Bee! Dat nigga ain't shit! I started to slump his ass! He pissed at me 'cause they Cuban connect named Fish got shot up and robbed for a lot of yay and jewelry. They murked his ass."

"Why he mad at you for that? Did you do it?" I asked and turned all the way around in my seat to look at him.

He just gave me a blank stare, then said, "Fuck ass Cuban tried to open up shop, playing both sides of the field, selling us Yayo and selling to the competition for a cheaper price, had niggas running 'round gunning at each other."

"So, you killed him?" I asked.

He just gave me a hard stare and then said, "He was one

of your dad's plugs. Me and Big Bee ain't been cool since." Mellow turned around, looking back at the safe.

"I have to get Big Bee out of jail," I said with a weary sigh.

"Dat nigga got a hundred-thousand-dollar bond. You'd need ten stacks for the bail bondsman to get him," Mellow said as he looked at the safe.

"Damn, I can't get that bitch opened," he muttered and scratched his head.

There was an AK-47 on the floor, showing from under the couch, and another pistol sticking out from the pillow cushion. *This is definitely Mellow's stash house,* I thought as I placed the nine on the table. Mellow was strapped to the T.

Miami had always been not just the cocaine capital of the United States but also number one for vicious murders and gangland slayings.

Suddenly, Mellow turned and placed his hand on my thigh. I had on a white Prada skirt and a pink silk blouse.

"You have to let me handle this situation with these niggas. I'm tellin' you now, both Steve and G are going to be a problem. You were supposed to be dead. They might still be trying to set you up and kill you."

I glanced down at his hand on my thigh and adamantly shook my head. "You might be right, but that is a chance I'm just going to have to take. As for them being a problem, they are my problem now. I just can't let them get away with what they did to my family and me. Don't you understand?" I shouted.

He removed his hand. "Kadisha, this shit is real! Niggaz dying like flies 'round dis bitch! You ain't built for this type of shit!"

I twisted my lips with pungent disdain for what he said. "I can't just sit around and wait for you to do something I can do for myself."

"Like what?"

"Like murder Steve after I make him tell me where my father is."

Mellow looked at me like I was crazy then threw both his hands up in the air in frustration.

"Are you fucking serious?"

"Yes, I'm dead serious! I have Steve wrapped around my baby finger. That nigga will do anything I say, trust me. If my father is still alive and Steve knows where he is, he will tell me," I confidently said.

"Man, you have lost yo' muthufuckin' mind! Dat nigga Steve on some grimy shit."

"And I'ma be a grimy bitch not giving a fuck! I lost everything I loved. Don't you understand me?" My voice quivered, and I willed myself not to cry again.

Mellow just looked at me with compassion and then shook his head like he couldn't believe me.

"Fuck!" he cursed, balling up his fist as he watched me dig into my Gucci handbag and take out my iPhone.

I put it on speaker and gestured for Mellow to be quiet as he looked at me with his mouth open like he suddenly had lock jaw.

Steve answered on the second ring.

"Hi, Steve. What you doing?" I sweetly said.

Mellow, with a stricken expression, began to wave his hands frantically. *"NO!"* He was desperately trying to convince me not to do it.

"Where you at?" Steve asked. I could hear music in the background.

"I'm at my aunt's house in Opa Locka, chilling," I lied.

"You want me to come get you?"

"No, not now. I want to meet with you someplace alone, just you and me. I'm sorry. I made a terrible mistake. I need you in my life. Whatever you want me to do, I'll do. Can you find it in your heart to forgive me?"

"Hell yeah, I can forgive you! How about I get a room for a week, just you and me? You let me make you my lady, officially." He beamed.

"Okay, but you have to take it easy with me. I'm still sort of like a virgin," I said, and then added, "I'll call you back when I'm ready."

"Hold up! Kadisha, did you find out anything about who did that fucked up shit to your family and you?" he asked. I could hear the edginess in his voice.

"No. The police say they have no leads, no suspects," I said. I held the phone tightly as my pulse raced.

"I'm sorry to hear that. You know I got my ear to the streets. If I hear anything, I'm on it," he said. The tone in his voice sounded relaxed.

"Uh, huh," I muttered into the phone, not trusting my voice. I looked over at Mellow; his jaw was clenched tight.

"What about dat fuck nigga Mellow?"

"What about him?"

"You fuckin' with him? What kind of shit was that you pulled at the hospital a while back?"

I glanced at Mellow. He was fuming mad, nostrils flaring like he wanted to punch me in my face.

"He's just a friend, boy," I said, rolling my eyes.

"Well, since he's just a friend, tell me where he lives," Steve said in a gritty tone.

"For what?" I asked and looked at Mellow.

He scowled at me with his lips pressed tight across his handsome face.

"Because, from what I'm hearing, dat nigga had something to do with the home invasion. I want to serve his ass proper this time."

Mellow began to make all kinds of contorted angry faces like he was about to go ballistic.

"Humph," I huffed into the phone as I subconsciously rubbed the gauze bandage on my head, trying to think of a good reply. I needed to rock Steve to sleep.

"I'll have the information for you when we meet at the hotel, okay."

I hung up the phone.

Mellow rushed me so fast I was certain he was going to hit me. Instead, he grabbed me by my shoulders and gently shook me.

"Listen, Kadisha, you see the kind of fuck shit this nigga sayin'? He's lying on me because he's desperate. You're supposed ta be dead. It's no tellin' what he'll try to do to you if he gets you alone. You gotta remember, you saw G's face. You're a witness to a horrific crime. You could be walking into a trap. Take me with you. Let me wet his fuck ass up," Mellow pleaded in one long breath. The diamonds in his grill sparkled.

I pulled away from him. I wasn't really listening to a word he said.

"I'm going to need that blowtorch and the gun I used to murk dude." I pointed at the small hand blowtorch that he had tried to open the safe with; my mind was plotting, conspiring.

"What da fuck for?" Mellow raised his voice.

I ignored him. My mind was on murder and revenge. I continued, "I'm also going home to get a change of clothes. I need a bath... and to get my thoughts together."

"You're damn right. You need to get your thoughts together, Kadisha, and let me handle this."

I moved away from him and spoke with passion, leading with my head and not my heart. "Let's get one thing straight. I recruited you. I'm placing you in a situation to come up. There is the safe and me. I'm offering you both, but under one condition."

"What's that?" he shot back.

"Let me lead. Let me deal with Steve. You can deal with Graylin Kelly for now."

"For now? Check this, Kadisha. You ain't listening to me. These niggaz is official goons. They play for keeps. They play with them choppers. It ain't as simple as you think. They'll kill you in a heartbeat—"

"I understand what you're saying... but I gotta do what I gotta do," I said with steel in my voice.

Mellow walked up close. I saw something wash over his face. I'm certain it was pity for me. He thought I had lost my damn mind. He took me into his arms and held me close. The moment lingered as he began to caress my back. He kissed me on my cheek, then my earlobe, as he held me in his arms. I can't lie; it felt good. I needed to be held.

"Okay, I can't stop you. But can you please tell me what you are going to do with a blow torch," he asked, speaking into the section of my hair that wasn't bandaged.

"I'm going to make him tell me where my daddy is," I confidently replied.

"There is the real possibility that your dad may not be alive," Mellow softly said and caressed my back, comforting me.

"Then... I want to bring his body home... to be buried. At least I will know, but I got to know... I gotta know," I said and nearly choked up.

"Okay, but there are so many other people involved. So many shady players. How can you know who to trust?"

"Like who?" I looked into his handsome eyes just as he slid his hand on my backside.

"Like your mom, your Aunt Esther, and Big Bee."

CHAPTER
Eighteen

Kadisha

He had a point about everybody but Big Bee. I was certain Bee didn't have anything to do with it. He had shot and killed one of the dudes. Plus, he had been with my father since I was about four years old.

Mellow then changed the subject back to the original topic.

"You call me if anything goes wrong. You hear me, Kadisha?" He raised his voice. For a second, I thought I saw fear in his eyes as he grabbed me and held me tight in his arms. He whispered barely audibly, "You gotta be careful. Chicks don't go up against these types of dudes... This is so dangerous what you're doing."

Silence, thoughts merged, death lingered, waiting for a verdict.

"In the meantime, try to think of the combination to the safe. It could be a partial phone number, an address, a birthdate, or anything. Your dad must have had something awfully important in there to make them take that big ass risk to come back for the safe."

He had a point. I had that gut feeling you always get when you're forgetting something, and you know it's there. I just couldn't place my finger on it. I tried to figure it out as I glanced over at the safe. Then, Mellow kissed me again. This time on my chin, soft as a feather. Then he kissed my neck and palmed my ass, squeezing it. I could feel his penis pressed against me. His sexual desire was strong, undeniably strong. I felt something stir deep inside me. Perhaps it was the weed or the feel of his hard body pressed against mine. He eased his hand under my skirt and tugged at my panties, causing me to breathe hard. I sucked in air. Instantly, I felt myself getting moist. Then, Mellow whispered in a sultry voice, brimming with desire.

"You said I could have you and the safe... well, all I really want... is you..." He eased my panties down to my thighs.

I nodded. This was all part of my plan, part of the sacrifice I was willing to make for the sake of what I needed to do. I was willing to be his chick because I needed him in the worst way. My body and that safe were all I had for the offering. Love wasn't the only theme; Mellow was my method to the madness.

He eased me down onto the couch. I sat next to a gun

stashed in the cushion. For some reason, I looked at the dead man, then closed my eyes and enjoyed my first high. Mellow's hands spread my legs. He grabbed my clitoris with his forefinger and thumb and caressed it like he was trying to start a fire between my legs. Then, ever so gently, he eased his middle finger inside my tight vagina, causing me to gasp and moan. The feeling was titillating. The whole time, he kissed me passionately. His tongue was sweet as licorice inside my mouth. Suddenly, I was hot and horny. So hot that I was melting right in his hands. I could feel my own juices running down my thighs. Then, Mellow eased another finger inside me as his tongue darted around in my mouth, playing tag with my tongue. Then, he slid it down my neck to my breasts, searching, licking, sucking. My hand, as if having a mind of its own, lifted my bra strap, and my breasts sprang free. He greedily sucked on my nipple, then tried to ease another finger inside me.

"Ouch..." I squirmed. I was too tight for three of his large fingers.

"I forget you ain't had much pipe," Mellow said in a husky voice brimming with sex while nibbling on my erect nipple.

Then, suddenly, he moved away. His lips and hands were absent from my body. He fumbled with his zipper; the sound was like a stuffed scream. It resonated in the room as I watched him reach down his leg and pull out his dick. It was like my high was playing some type of crude joke. Mellow's dick was long. A foot long and crooked as hell. It was three shades darker than the rest of his body, with its doorknob shaped head that was another shade lighter.

Then, his phone rang again. He frowned. I felt his leg jerk in frustration, and in the middle of our passionate prologue to sex, my female instinct told me that Mellow had a chick. I was certain of it. Not just that, he had a big ole dick!

Bug-eyed, I stared, mouth agape. He had just ruined the mood.

I heard him chuckle lightly. "Gone touch it," he said.

"Uh, uh, boy, your dick too big. I'm still a virgin, kinda. You ain't putting that thang in me and tearin' up my insides. Besides, who is that chick who keeps blowing up your phone?" I complained.

Technically, I was sort of a virgin and not used to dudes and their whorish ways. As for the intimacy with a dude, I had never willingly had sex. I had been raped, and Mellow's dick was bigger than both dudes' dicks that had raped me put together. He had just created a major problem, like a coochie dilemma.

"I'ma just put the head in. Here, touch it," he persuaded, aiming his dick at me and placing his hand on the back of my neck, nudging me forward like he expected me to suck his dick.

Ugggh, I think not!

But still, hesitantly, call it my feminine curiosity, I reached out and took hold of his dick with enough room left for three more hands. I couldn't even get my fingers around it as I felt it pulsate and throb. He looked at me with eager eyes, thirsty for my sex. On the other side of the room was the dead body, my induction into the life. High off weed, with the threat of a big penis penetrating me, it should have been exciting, but I just wasn't ready.

"Dawg, you got a big ole dick," I said, speaking aloud to myself. I was still high off the weed, and his dick looked enormous.

He leaned forward, spread my legs, and sucked on my breasts as he pushed me back onto the couch. His hands were everywhere at once, fast, with the expertise of a true thug. *He is prepared to ravish my body,* I thought as I listened to his heavy breathing.

"You said I could have you. You said you were going to be my lady." He eased on top of me, spreading my thighs. I could feel his dick, hard as wood, pressing onto my vagina's entrance, nudging, prodding, and probing.

"Hold up, wait!" I screeched with the palms of my hands pressed against his muscular chest. He was deter-mined to get his dick in me.

Steve's slow ass would have never been this aggressive, but in the craziest way, Mellow was turning me on. It just dawned on me that I was not ready, not yet.

"I told you, I'ma just put the head in," Mellow grum-bled, and he began to squeeze my breasts, licking and slob-bering all over them, trying to enter me.

Some kind of way, we ended up in an awkward, crazy position with both his feet on the floor, his pants around his ankles, and my leg over his shoulder. He was aggressive, rough even. I should have been offended, but I wasn't.

"Stop... get... up."

He wouldn't stop, and I continued to weakly resist. Finally, he got the head in, and it hurt like hell. Involuntarily, I hollered. My seventeen-year-old body wasn't prepared for this. I scooted away, and his dick came out.

"Fuck, what you doin'?" Mellow yelled, showing me one of his angry sex faces. He placed his hand around my waist, trying to pin me to the couch.

Again, his phone rang.

"You not putting that thang in me. I'm not ready. Besides, you need a condom."

"Condom?" He frowned like somebody had just run over his foot with a car. "A condom for what? To ruin all this good pussy? Stop playin', gurl."

He continued trying to enter me. His dick was like a blind man, bumping into all the wrong places, including my butt.

"Ouch, wrong hole. Get up, I ain't playin', boy."

I pushed him off me, pressing my knee into his chest. He rolled over onto the floor. I hopped up and stood, stepping over him. He tried to grab my leg but was too slow. I scooped up my panties off the floor. The moment was almost comical.

"Oh, you gon' try a nigga like that? What, you into dick teasing? Now, if I take dat phat pussy, you'd think a nigga dead ass wrong," Mellow threatened, getting up off the floor and walking toward me.

For a minute, I was overwhelmed with fear as I watched him. He wrestled to place his ramrod hard dick back into his pants. His eyes were bloodshot red as he glowered at me. I glanced over at the gun on the table.

"I'm sorry, Mellow... I just can't do it right now," I timidly said, taking a step back.

He must have read my thoughts. He took a second to compose himself, and I heard a whistle of breath through his nose as he expelled a deep sigh. He tore his eyes away from me, and his expression changed. His sex face was replaced with the gentler, kinder person I knew.

"Okay, okay, we good. I understand..." he said, nodding his head.

His hand was still on his dick in his pants. For some reason, he was squeezing it as if he was trying to bend it or maybe make it go down.

Then, out of the blue, he placed a comforting hand on my shoulder, rubbing it. That was a compassionate habit of his, just like my father used to do. And, as crazy as it may sound, Mellow reminded me a lot of my father. They were both ruthless thugs with a soft side to them.

Again, he shifted the big dick bulge around in his pants. He walked away and untied the dead dude. Shoving his body into the plastic he had on the floor, he landed with a thump. I watched as he wrapped the body up like a mummy. The guy still had a pained scowl on his face. Even in death, I could see his torment.

As I watched, something horrible dawned on me. All my life, I had been subconsciously prepared for death and murder. I had seen so much growing up in Miami's notorious Pork and Beans projects; the dead guy was just another facet of life that I intended to fully portray from watching my father and his ways. Like it or not, I was a gangstas' daughter.

"I'ma take this nigga to Alligator Alley and feed him to the gators," Mellow said, playing off the fact that had I been another chick, there was a real possibility he would have taken the coochie.

I was in deep thought as I watched him drag the dude toward the door, and then I realized what he'd just said.

Alligator Alley is a long stretch of wild, deserted land, like a swamp out in the middle of nowhere, full of alligators and poisonous snakes in the South Florida Everglades.

"I'm going to need a car to drive home to get my clothes and take a shower. After I finish with Steve, I'll be back. "

"You can use the Charger. Niggaz don't know it's my whip. Dat's the reconnaissance mobile. What I use to come through doin' the smooth creep. The keys are over there on the table." He gestured, then demurred. "Kadisha, can I go with you? That nigga Steve ain't right."

His words fell on deaf ears. I ignored his question as I walked over and kissed him on the bridge of his nose. He grabbed me around my waist with firm hands; he was so unpredictable.

For some reason, I spoke in a rushed tone. "I wasn't tryin' to play you. There is a right time and place for everything. I'm going to give you some... I promise. It's just that I've got so much on my mind. I've been through too much," I sincerely said.

He just looked at me with brown eyes that were hard to read. I turned and scooped up the keys off the table. On my way to the door, I picked up the propane blow torch. It was one of those miniature things, but it was heavier than it looked.

"Kadisha!" he called.

Startled, I stalled. With my hand on the doorknob, I turned around and looked at him with a penetrating stare. Then I looked at the safe that possessed only God knows what.

Mellow continued, "I sho hope you know what the fuck you doing!"

His words were like a slap in my face as I thought, *I hope I know what I'm doing, too,* and walked out the door to an unknown fate.

CHAPTER Nineteen

Mellow

As soon as Kadisha walked out the door, I resisted the urge to run after her. I needed to try to stop her, to tell her that she was out of her league, out of her bounds. But I knew, just like her dad, she was stubborn as hell, the kind of chick who was born a leader, not a follower. She wouldn't have listened.

I walked over and looked at the safe again, but I couldn't keep my thoughts off Kadisha. The sway of her hips, her sensuous thighs, her delicate breasts, and her beautiful smile had me hypnotized. I had done everything in my power to fuck her. I really wanted to get into those panties. Kadisha had a banging ass body, ass for days, and a slim waist. I knew it should have been money over bitches with her. But, to be honest, she had a nigga fucked up from day one.

When I used to see her at school, strutting with that phat ass, I knew one day she'd be mine. She always dressed fly and rocked the latest gear. She hung out with a gang of bad chicks, too. But what made her stand out the most was that she was a real trooper and had a boss bitch swagger. However, when she murked dude in my living room, cold as ice, that sealed the deal.

I had to respect her gangsta. I saw something in her eyes that sent a chill down my spine. I couldn't deny her the plea-sure of killing Steve. She came from a gangsta's lineage; her pops was that nigga! I knew firsthand that he had helped a graveyard flourish, replenishing it with niggas who he and Big Bee had personally sent to their eternal resting place.

As I marinated on my thoughts of Kadisha, I couldn't help noticing that the dead man wrapped in plastic seemed to stare at something only his blood smeared eyes could see. Absentmindedly, I sniffed my fingers; the scent of Kadisha's pussy lingered. Instantly, I got an erection again. I consid-ered jacking my dick while imagining her with her legs wrapped around my waist, titties jiggling as she bounced on my dick, but I decided against it.

Unbeknownst to her, she had placed me in a fucked up situation. She dropped a nuclear bomb on me when she said my cousin G, whose government name was Graylin Kelly, was one of the dudes who raped her and did all those terrible things to her family. G was the kind of dude who inspired awe and fear in everybody because of his reputa-tion. It was going to be difficult to step to him. Still, I didn't want to believe it. Pondering the situation, I reached over and fired up the partial blunt that was on the table as I looked at the safe and the dead dude on the floor next to the door.

What the fuck am I going to do next? I thought as I rubbed my dick. Kadisha was trying to give a nigga blue balls on top of all that. My mind was all over the place. Then, I heard Kadisha start the Charger. I listened to the engine purr as it rumbled. I got up, walked over to the window, and caught a glimpse of Kadisha as she mashed out.

"Fuck!" This had to be one of the worst days of my life.

I turned away from the window and glanced back at the safe. For some reason, my cousin G kept creeping into my mind, making me sick to my stomach.

Graylin Kelly, my cousin, was nothing short of a genius. He could have entered college on an academic scholarship or even for sports. He had the physique for it, and colleges around the nation had been trying to recruit him since his sophomore year at Miami High School when he took them to the national state championship as the quarterback and won.

At six foot three, G was cut up like he had been lifting weights all his life. He was shiny and black as night. He wore his hair short in a Caesar cut with beehive waves. Some said he resembled Michael Vick, the football player. He also had hands of steel. He was known for knocking niggas out cold, especially older dudes who had reps in the hood. G wanted to claim their reputations as part of his ghetto rise to fame in the hood.

G's mama, my aunt, Tasha Graylin, better known as Sexy Red in the strip clubs, had exposed him to a lifestyle like no other. All she dated were dope boys, ballers, and hustlers who were getting major paper—young millionaires. It was hard for G not to be attracted to the lavish lifestyles of her boyfriends. All of them used to spoil G with money and dope. It seemed that they were grooming him for the illicit trade of cocaine, considering Miami is the cocaine capital of the United States.

By the time G was twelve, he was hustling hard on the block with my aunt's approval. He bought his first whip at thirteen, an old Chevy Caprice, and tricked it out with candy apple red paint, twenty-six-inch rims, and a banging sound system. He caught his first body when he was fifteen. He robbed Haitian Fred for ten birds and six hundred thousand dollars. At the time, Haitian Fred was dating his mama, Sexy Red.

One thing about G is he didn't drink or smoke. His only habit was gambling. Other than that, all he did was plot and connive on how to come up. My auntie Tasha loved it. In fact, she was the mastermind behind some of the capers G used to pull off. It was as if they were both addicted to power. By the time he was twenty, I was only sixteen. In real years, four years didn't make much of a difference, but in the streets years, it was a lifetime of valuable knowledge and experience that directly correlated with life and death wrapped up in those four years.

Graylin Kelly formed his infamous clique, the John Doe Boys, at the age of twenty, and the rest was history. They were murderers, slaughtering everybody, even bitches, over drug wars and turf. The last murder that I had personally known of was an OG named Day-Day. He was killed about a week after he came home from the feds.

Day-Day was much older than G. Before he left to serve ten years of fed time, he had a booming trap on 25th. They specialized in selling parlay dime rocks to hustlers. You had to buy fifty or more. The cocaine rocks were so big that a hustler could break them down and triple their money to get their hustle on. It was a brilliant idea, and Day-Day made millions selling dime rocks that way. The thing was, when he came back home to his block in Liberty City, things had changed. Graylin Kelly wasn't even allowed off the front porch back then, but now Graylin was running the entire Liberty City with his goons, the John Doe Boys. They had a vicious reputation for putting in work.

The first week that Day-Day was out, he opened up shop with a new connect and an old hustle: the parlay dime rock game. Well, he *attempted* to open up shop, but Graylin and several of his dudes swooped down on Day-Day's workers, robbed them at gunpoint, and pistol-whipped them, taking all their dope. The next night, Day-Day made the crucial mistake of retaliating. In a badly planned attempt to ambush and murder G and two of his henchmen as they drove on the expressway from the strip club, Day-Day's crew rolled up right next to them and opened fire. They riddle G's vehicle with automatic weapons, causing the Lexus SUV to swerve and crash into the median. However, G only sustained minor injuries and a fractured wrist. No one else was harmed. Soon, the streets started talking, and the word was that Day-Day and G were at war.

Two nights later, Day-Day sat in his Benz that was parked in front of Big Booty Brenda's house in the projects. Brenda had just given birth to an infant son. The father was locked up, and she was in need of money, pampers, and infant formula, which cost a fortune. Day-Day was the only answer to her financial problems, and it just so happened he was trying to talk his way into her panties. He offered her a large wad of cash and some coke for her nose-candy habit. It was an offer she had trouble refusing, even though she thought he was fat and ugly.

The baby cried nonstop on her lap in the smoke-filled car as they listened to music. Brenda pretended to ponder Day-Day's generous offer to pay for a hotel room for a week and a babysitter, as well as give her a stack and all the cocaine she could snort. That would give her a chance to get out of her momma's house for a brief vacation and get high for free.

Unfortunately, neither Day-Day nor Brenda ever saw the black Yukon SUV with smoked black tinted windows and its lights off as it eased behind them on the other side of the nearly deserted street. The baby continued to cry as four gunmen exited the vehicle dressed in all black, wearing ski masks, and armed with AK-47s. They calmly walked up to the car with G leading the way; this was his forte.

"Yeah, nigga what's up?" G said with a snarl under the mask.

Startled, Day-Day looked up and jerked his neck. The barrel of the AK-47 was aimed straight at his dome. He flinched to go for his strap, but it was too late. The first shot blew the top of his head off. It also struck nineteen-year-old Brenda in her chest. From then on, a barrage of bullets struck the car, killing Day-Day, Brenda, and her infant son. It was a gruesome murder scene.

Soon after, the FBI decided to start an overt investigation of Graylin Kelly and his notorious John Doe Boys. For the second time that year, the infamous John Doe Boys had made it onto a segment of the popular TV show *The First 48*.

The only reason I was privy to so much information about this particular horrific scene was that I was one of the masked gunmen. I didn't know there was a baby in the car until it was too late. The next day, I saw it on the news, and the thought of it still haunts me. As for G, he didn't give a fuck; he was on a power trip.

I have a tattoo of a baby in a casket on my arm with the letters RIP. No one knows what that tat is for. All I can say is that gangstas have hearts, too.

I PLOPPED down on the couch and accidentally sat on the Glock 40 that was stashed in the cushion. I had gats galore stashed everywhere in the old house, and for good reason. Everyone I knew who was my age and hustling wound up either dead or in prison before they were twenty-five years old. It was just a facet of life in the ecology of the ghetto where I lived. I'd already been to prison, so I was determined to elude a fate that was likely predestined for me, as if the Grim Reaper followed me everywhere I went.

I sat on the couch and pondered what to do next. I tried to chase the image of Kadisha out of my mind. Then, suddenly, on a whim, I decided to call my cousin G. I knew I was no match for him, but I had to confront him. I wasn't a punk, and I fully intended to find out the truth. I had to know if he was one of the culprits who committed that failed ass home invasion.

Perhaps there was a mistake; maybe it wasn't him.

Perhaps...

I dialed his number. It rang nonstop, and I waited. I looked over at the cast-iron, indestructible safe that had been impossible to penetrate. I had beat on that bitch with a sledgehammer, even used a blow torch, and still couldn't get it open. Again, I wondered just what could possibly be stored inside it. After all, the safe belonged to Ike Spencer, one of the most notorious gangsta, kingpin niggas in Miami. There may have even been a clue as to where he was. It could be a treasure trove of shit in it, and I intended to find out.

Just as I was about to hang up the phone, G answered.

"What's up, cousin?" he said in a throaty baritone.

"Nuttin', just checking on you. You good?" I said, feeling my pulse race like I was about to have an anxiety attack.

"Nawl, I ain't good. What's up with you and Steve? He said he bitch slapped you, took your sack and money, and shot up your whip with the 9mm. Now you running around spreading lies n' shit on him—"

"That fuck nigga lying!" I sprang up from the couch. My blood was boiling. "I'm the one bitch slapped him and took his dope 'cause he set up my nigga—"

"Fuck you talkin' 'bout? Where you at, nigga?" he asked, cutting me off. It sounded like I heard muffled sounds in the background. He was whispering something to his crew as he held his hand over the phone. Then, he said, "We were just about to come see you."

WE? His words resonated in my head.

"I'm at da crib. What da business is, yo?" I asked and felt my heart beating faster in my chest like the Grim Reaper was standing over me already.

"Yo, cousin, where you stayin' at in The Grove nowadays?" he asked.

I held on to the Glock so tight it hurt my hand.

"I'm... I'm... I've been trappin' out of hotels n' shit. Ain't really staying in no particular place these days. Still on my grind. Why?" I lied.

G ain't never wanted to know where I lived. Yes, we were blood, but I knew without a shadow of a doubt that he would kill me without a second thought if he felt I threatened him in any way.

"All them licks you been hitting, nigga. Plus, we just broke major bread with the last lick, and you staying in hotels? Get the fuck outta here." G scoffed.

The lick he was talking about was the Cuban named Fish. He was also Big Bee's plug. He had been trying to play both sides of the field, selling yay to both sets of enemies for different prices. It caused a big rift. Fish always tried to act black, flaunting in different exotic half-million-dollar whips with bad ass bitches. He did everything in his power to fit in, but I could see through that shit. He was only fucking with us for the money. He really thought that all the niggas he was selling dope to were dumb because, although he was warned not to sell dope to the competition, he still did it behind our backs. To me, he was nothing but a rich ass Cuban dude trying to get over.

Fish was smart, though. He had a foolproof plan of how not to get jacked. He always conducted business in the crowded mall, so a nigga couldn't touch his ass. He was partially correct until G recruited me. I robbed and shot him in broad daylight when he tried to buck in the Miami Mall parking lot as we sat in his Mercedes truck. I took ten kilos of dope, a phat ass iced out gold chain, and his platinum and diamond Rolex watch.

G had set the lick up. He got eight kilos, and my cut was two. I wasn't stupid. I knew the only reason G recruited me for the job was that I was young and wild; I didn't give a fuck. Plus, when I came home, I was on my dick, doing bad.

"We got some shit going on that I need to holla at you about. Stop by the Island Apartments. I need to see you within the hour, or I'ma come your way. Na'mean?" G finally said.

I felt my stomach knot up and churn with butterflies. G was up to something.

"What you need to talk to me about? And what's up wit' dat nigga Steve? I'm telling you, that fuck nigga ain't right," I said with grit, trying to keep a calm voice as I held the Glock like I was about to start shooting.

"Mell, I don't play the phone. Feel me? Just come, nigga. Ya startin' to make a nigga feel some kinda way."

Threat.

"Okay... okay... I need to first go drop something off," I said, thinking about the body wrapped in plastic. "I'll be there within an hour."

I hung up the phone, feeling some type of way. It sounded like G was siding with Steve, and maybe he had good reason to. If they were behind the home invasion on Kadisha's family, there was a strong chance that I could be walking into a trap.

What does G want with me? I continued to ask myself.

I would soon find out, and by then, it would be too late.

I GOT UP, walked down the hall to my bedroom, grabbed a sixteen shot 9mm and a 40 caliber, and stuffed both of them shits in my waistband. I also took two and a half ounces of *hard jugglers* for the junkies on the avenue to give my lieutenant, Lil Will.

I headed out the door, preparing for the inevitable: my confrontation with G. The Grim Reaper was right on my shoulder.

CHAPTER
Twenty

Mellow

I drove to The Grove. It was only a few miles away from the stash house I'd just left. As I drove down 22nd Street, headed for my trap, I spotted Lil Willy with a chick posted up in front of our trap house. They were leaning against his tricked-out, customized, Canary-yellow and orange '64 Chevy. The car was Miami Hurricane football colors, sitting on 26-inch rims. Like everyone else in the city, Lil Willy was a true Hurricane fan.

"S'up, nigga?" I said as I rolled up.

Instantly, I recognized the chick he was with—a hood rat named Poochie. She was hard to miss with her big ole donkey ass. She had on some black skin-tight pants that looked like tights and a short, see-through blouse that showed off her navel ring and some type of butterfly tattoo.

"Heyyyyy, Mell," she cajoled. She wore flaming red hair weave that blended in perfectly with her freckled cinnamon complexion. I ignored her. The truth was, I had hit, and the pussy wasn't all that.

"S'up wit' you, nigga?" Lil Willy replied and waved at Poochie like she was an annoying fly.

He bobbed over to my whip with his pants sagging so low that I could see the gat in his waistband. Then, suddenly, he thought about something, turned back around, and picked up his Styrofoam cup of lean off the ground.

I reached into my drawers and passed him the bomb of rocks.

"Give these to Nook. I want you to ride over to Liberty City to go holla at G and them niggas about some fuck shit."

Lil Willy didn't even blink an eye. To any other nigga, it would have cause for concern.

All he said was, "Aight," and walked away from the car. I could see the Tec-9 semi-automatic pistol he was carrying. He was always ready for action.

Lil Willy was only fifteen years old, with the heart of a lion. He didn't give a fuck. Before I recruited him and his brother, Nook, to work on my team, the two of them had been robbing tourists in Miami and eating good doing it. That was one of the best hustles in the MIA. What people don't know is that the average tourist carries a large wad of cash. Most of them are foreigners and don't speak good English, which makes them perfect for the taking.

Lil Willy and Nook ended up shooting a tourist and

making the hustle hot for a lot of niggas. Many of those niggas were loyal to that hustle and had been using tourist jacking to make a living for years, from generation to generation. The homies wanted to whack Lil Willy and his older brother, Nook, when I stepped in. I promised to keep them under my wing. The two brothers were always into something.

Lil Willy hopped into my whip. Preparing to ride shotgun, he placed the Tec-9 on his lap, balanced a cup of lean in the other hand, and passed me the previous night's sales money.

"Shit was gravy. Here's nine stacks," he said, passing me a brown paper bag full of cash. Then, he asked, "You straight, my nigga?"

"I dunno, I'ma see. Dat fuck nigga Steve done got wit' my cousin, G, tryna spray a nigga's name wit' some bullshit."

"See man, toldja we shoulda wet dat fuck nigga up dat day we caught him at Kadisha's house when we had his ass pent," Lil Willy said with a frown.

He wore his hair nappy, matted to his head. It gave him a menacing, roughneck appearance. Trust me when I say his looks were not deceiving. He really had mental issues.

"I know, but the old lady came out."

"Sheit, dat bitch dead now."

"Yeah, and I just found out that Steve and my cousin G might be behind that foul shit."

"Damnnnnn," Lil Willy droned, looking at me in disbelief.

"How did you find out?" he asked and took a sip from his cup.

"I caught some nigga coming out of Kadisha's crib, shot 'em, and put him in the trunk. The nigga's name was Mike or something... anyway, he told me everything. He said Steve and G was involved in the lick, or he lied to me. So, I'm finna find out now."

"You know them Liberty City niggas be on dat bullshit. They think I robbed Tat-Tat. Is you strapped?"

"Shit! I forgot all about that. I'ma take you back 'cause Tat is G's lieutenant, and there might be some shit."

"Fuck that. Don't take me back. That nigga didn't see me rob him. He shouldn't come to the club fronting with all dat jewelry, drunk and disrespecting the home team, na'mean. It was twenty niggas kicking his ass. He can't say it was me. You strapped, ain't you?"

It had completely slipped my mind that Lil Willy was beefing with them niggas. Two days later, Tat-Tat came back and shot up the club, killing one of the homies. However, I had to admit, like Lil Willy said, nobody saw him, so I continued to drive.

Big mistake.

"Hell yeah, nigga. I got two burners on me. Why?"

"'Cause I don't give a fuck. If them niggas act up, I'ma start dumping on they ass," Lil Willy said, then reached under his shirt and pulled out one of the prettiest silver and black nine millimeters I'd ever seen.

"Where'd you get that?"

"Junkie sold it to me for nine rocks last night."

"Nigga, lemme buy it from you. It was my dope you bought it with," I said, looking at the gun.

"Get the fuck outta here."

We both laughed.

Lil Wily took a sip from the cup. The liquid was deep purple; there was probably three or four hundred dollars' worth of lean in that little ass cup.

AFTER WE DISPOSED of the body in the trunk, silence enveloped us like a black cloud as I drove to Liberty City. Periodically, I looked into my mirror with vigilance. I didn't want to get caught slipping. I also checked my cell phone again to see if I had missed any messages from Kadisha. She still had not called me. All the calls were from a couple of chicks.

One in particular was from a chick named Ebony. I had been beating in her guts for a minute, me and just about every other nigga that was getting money. Ebony was nothing more than a side bitch who knew how to play her position. A nigga didn't mind breaking her off something proper for a shot of ass because she had some good ass pussy and some smoking head. But, lately, the chick had been damn near stalking me, blowing up my phone. The ironic thing was that she had fucked my cousin, G, too.

IT WAS nightfall when we rolled up in Liberty City. There was a full moon in the sky. The night looked eerie and gloomy. For some reason, there wasn't much street activity.

In my mind, I had been struggling to figure out just how I was going to confront my cousin, G. Also, I had been stalking my phone for a text message or call from Kadisha. As I drove through the plush, rich white folks' section of town, doing a slow creep, Lil Willy silently rode shotgun with the Tec-9 on his lap. To the unsuspecting eye, Liberty City looked like something out of a rich and famous glamor magazine with its elegant splendor. Bentleys and Maybachs lined the driveways of the half-million-dollar homes.

As we drove deeper into the heart of the city, into the Black section, I could feel the hair on the back of my neck stand up. Dope fiends walked the streets like zombies in a trance, along with hustlers and prostitutes. Lil Willy, as if sensing trouble, had slid all the way down in the seat, gripping the Tec-9 securely in his hand.

I pulled up in front of the trap that G ran with his crew, The John Doe Boys. They had the entire Island Apartments on lock. The building was nearly a block long, with about two thousand impoverished people living there. It was mostly Section 8 housing, like a big ass project.

I parked next to the dumpster in the parking lot out front. Like any trap, the lookouts spotted us immediately. There were dudes shooting dice in front of the building, lots of night activity, and the streetlights had been shot out. I had a terrible feeling as I fanned away a couple of curious crackheads. Then, out of nowhere, this thick chick appeared. She was strutting with wavy, undulating hips swaying from side to side. Her white, skin-tight, coochie-cutter short-shorts had all her ass hanging out. She had a camel toe, pussy for days. She was caramel complected, like one of her parents was white. Her long hair was styled, cascading over the right side of her breasts. She wasn't wearing a bra, and her nipples looked as big as headlights.

"Can I go with y'all?" she flirted in a sing-song voice.

Placing her hand on her round hip, she made her breasts bounce as she strutted toward us. That's when I noticed she was pigeon-toed and bowlegged, fine as shit. She had us both awestruck.

"Yeah! Hell yeah! You can come!" Lil Willy said, sitting straight up in his seat.

I ain't gon' lie. I seriously thought about smashing ole

girl; she had a phat ass. But then something caught my attention in my peripheral, some type of movement. Just as I turned to look, there was a gun placed to my head, and two niggaz jumped from behind the dumpster, aiming choppers at me and Lil Willy. The bitch took off running. Lil Willy came up with the Tec-9... too late.

We'd been set up by one of the oldest tricks in the book —a bitch with a pretty smile and a banging body.

CHAPTER
Twenty-One

Mellow

"Fuck nigga, I should splatter yo' ass right here!" the gritty baritone voice threatened as the cold steel was pressed tightly against my temple.

I would have recognized that voice anywhere; it belonged to my cousin, G. Across from me, in the passenger seat, Lil Willy was frozen, with the cup of lean in one hand and the Tec-9 in the other.

"So, this how you get down on me, cousin?" I asked, trying to keep the nervous edge out of my voice. The dudes who were shooting dice stopped what they were doing. My hand was still on my nine. I was about to come up firing.

Then, the gat was moved from my head, and I heard a dry chuckle as G responded, "I'm just letting you know we gangstas over here, and a nigga will get bodied if he comes through here wit' dat fuck shit." He chuckled.

G always had a fucked-up sense of humor, and that night wasn't any different. His flunkies, fat ass E-class, Mike Dee, K-9, and Bam, along with a couple of other dudes that I didn't know, laughed as if G had just told the funniest joke in the world. The thing with G was he did things for a reason. He was careful and conniving, even if just to gain a psychological advantage. His mind was meticulous. We once got kicked out of a Vegas gambling casino; they accused him of counting cards. But, by then, he had already won over three hundred thousand just playing Blackjack.

"Man, you play too muhfuckin' much," I said, upset.

My hand was still on the burner on my lap as my heart pounded in my chest. He didn't know I had come within seconds of blasting on his ass.

I heard Lil Willy grumble, "Mane, y'all niggaz wit' dat fuck shit!"

Across the street, I saw the bitch who had walked over to the car. She was standing with the crowd of dudes at the building breezeway, watching us.

"Y'all get out the car. Follow me," G commanded.

I didn't like his tone of voice.

Then I heard one of G's henchmen, a dude named Bam, say, "Hey, that's Lil Willy in the car! That's Lil Willy in the car! Somebody go get Tat-Tat."

"Lil Willy?" G echoed and bent down, looking at the passenger seat. Then, he said, "What you bring him for?"

"That's my little nigga. Why? What y'all tripping 'bout?" I asked, playing dumb.

"Yeah, what the fuck wrong wit' y'all?" Willy scoffed, playing it off.

"Dat nigga was wit dat bullshit the night Tat-Tat got jumped. They took his jewelry," Mike Dee instigated.

"Dig, cousin, we didn't come all the way here for no drama," I said to downplay the situation.

"Nigga, I ain't have nothin' ta do wit dat bullshit," Lil Willy snapped. By then, he had his hand on his strap, and the moment became volatile all over again, ready to erupt with violence. There were choppers still pointed at my whip.

"Tat-Tat! Yo, Tat-Tat, come here!" Mike D called out.

"If Tat come and say he got a problem with Lil Willy, then it's on," G threatened and stepped closer to the car.

"Man... fuck!" I cursed.

Moments later, Tat-Tat walked up with Mike Dee all in his ear, boosting him up to do some fuck shit.

Tat-Tat looked into the car and frowned, then pulled out his strap, a chrome-plated nine.

"Yeah, y'all fuck niggas jumped on me. What's up now, nigga?!" Tat-Tat swung the pistol to hit Lil Willy and missed.

Lil Willy ducked and was about to come up with the Tec-9, fully intent on blazing Tat-Tat. I grabbed his arm in the nick of time.

"Nawl, man!!" That was when I heard the staccato of

the assault weapons being cocked and loaded. They were getting ready to dump on us.

"Come on, man. I brought him with me. We s'posed ta be fam," I said to G with a plea in my voice.

G just looked at me for a moment as if considering what I said, and then he threw up his hands.

"Hold up! Hold up, man!!" G shouted. "Chill, Tat, give the nigga a pass. Plus, I have to admit his little ass got mad heart," G said with a chuckle.

I thought I saw him wink his eye at Tat-Tat. I hoped I was wrong.

"G, them niggaz jumped me!" Tat-Tat vented with Mike Dee nodding his head at his side.

Mike Dee had an AK-47, and everybody knew he was trigger happy. He was a skinny ass nigga who couldn't fight a lick but put a gun in his hands, and it was a different story.

"Nigga, I ain't touch yo' fuck ass." Lil Willy gritted. He was not making matters any better. It was like he had a death wish.

"Oh, your little ass wanna act hard?" Tat-Tat said and was about to shoot Lil Willy

"Hold up, man. I said chill. Y'all niggaz hurry up and get to the Lafayette and handle that business, then come back," G ordered.

Tat-Tat whined like a little kid. "Man, that's some bull-shit. Them niggaz jumped on me and stomped me out at da club." They walked off and got into a black Camaro.

"Lemme holla at you for a second, my nigga. And bring killa with you," G said to me with a grin.

I exchanged wary glances with Willy. He gave me a shrug like, 'whatever.' He placed the Tec-9 in his drawers, grabbed his cup of lean, took a sip, and bounced out of the car before me.

WE ENTERED the dilapidated apartment with six of G's goons. They were all mean-mugging us and walking close. The tension was high. The apartment smelled of crack smoke, funk, and stale cigarettes. There were several old chairs and a couch. From somewhere, a radio blared. Our feet echoed on the wooden floors as we walked to the kitchen. There was a table and several chairs.

A woman in her forties entered behind us. She gave us excited looks as she began to move around, all antsy, rubbing the palms of her hands on her pants. Then she began to clean the table for us. She was a dark complected woman in her forties with gray hair knotted up on her head and a scarf wrapped around it, like a headband. When she wiped the table and picked up an ashtray, I noticed the caked-up dirt under her fingernails. The tips of her fingers were burnt from smoking, and she smelled horrible.

When she spoke, her voice was polished, like maybe she used to be a schoolteacher or some type of professional. Crack didn't discriminate. No matter what she used to be, she had fallen victim to the drug.

"G, Tat-Tat, and 'nem ain't been giving me shit. Y'all be selling all day out my house and bringing them nasty girls in here fuckin' 'em," the woman complained as she nervously moved her hands.

"I got you as soon as they come back," G said, ignoring her.

The woman just stood there and looked at G. Her body went stiff like she was about to protest. G caught her drift, reached into his pocket, removed a bomb of rocks, and gave her a fifty-dollar slab rock. It was about the size of a matchbox and as thin as four quarters stacked together.

She smiled and got all animated like she was going to do a dance. "Thank you, baby," she said and scurried off.

It wasn't until G stepped into the light that I saw the jagged, ugly scratch running down the side of his face. I couldn't help but stare at it as I thought of Kadisha fighting for her life. She must have used every ounce of strength in her body to dig into G's face; he would definitely be scarred for life.

We were all crowded into the room like the forty thieves. I had a terrible vibe. So did Lil Willy; I could tell when he stole a glance at me. His hand was on the burner under his shirt. Plus, I knew he had the other gat on him.

Several of G's dudes just stood around, watching us, as if waiting for something to pop off.

E-Class was one of G's lieutenants. He was a big, black dude with dookie locks in his hair and a pot belly. He had a gravelly, deep voice that rattled like a two-pack-a-day smoker. He was part Haitian and crazy as fuck. A few weeks earlier, he and the John Doe Boys had run up in Rah-Rah's best friend's mother's birthday party and killed the mother and Rah-Rah's best friend, Shawn, just out of spite to get back at Rah-Rah.

E-Class sat at the table, oblivious to everyone else, and began to build a blunt. He took out two different bags of white powder and some weed.

"Dayum, my nigga, look at the rocks in dis bitch," he exclaimed as he held the bag up to the light. It was a half-ounce of Molly. The other bag contained cocaine. As E-Class carefully rolled the blunt with his tongue hanging out of his mouth in deep concentration, the room suddenly got quiet.

Unexpectedly, G said something that sent chills down my spine. "First off, if you strapped, place your burners on the table."

"What?! Come on, man. What kinda shit is dat?" I raised my voice.

G was supposed to be my cousin. We used to sleep on the same pissy ass mattress in the projects. You only ask dudes to do that kinda shit when you're getting ready to try some shady shit.

"If it's like that, my nigga, I'll wait in the car," Lil Willy said, making up an excuse to bounce.

As he turned and headed for the door, K-9 pressed the barrel of a 40. cal in his chest and pushed him back.

I looked at G as if to say, "What's going on?"

"Yeah, it's like that, and I ain't gon' ask you niggaz no more. Place your burners on the table!"

Lil Willy and I hesitated because to give up your burner was the truest form of getting bitched up and worse.

E-Class watched our verbal exchange like he was watching a volleyball game. He casually licked on the blunt like it was food; his eyes were lidded with larceny. He suddenly reached into his pants, took out a big ole Desert Eagle 44. and slammed it on the table so hard the table rattled. It may have seemed innocent, but it was intimidating.

"My nigga, this shit ain't hard. But if you niggas come up in this bitch stuntin', y'all gon' leave out this bitch stankin'. See, I'm leading by example." E-Class grinned, and the gold grill in his mouth looked like rusty copper. He was so fat that when he breathed, it sounded like he was snoring.

We continued to delay.

G nodded at two of his henchmen. Bam and some other nigga walked up and pulled out "sticks" from their pants (AK-47s).

Outmanned and overpowered, Lil Willy and I exchanged cautious glances. As if reading my mind, Lil

Willy reached into his pants and placed the Tec-9 on the table. I followed suit with my nine.

"See, that wasn't hard," G haughtily said and nodded to his dudes. They fell back with the sticks.

The entire time, I looked at him with pure hatred in my eyes.

"My nigga, this was not meant for you. Just fall back, cousin. You're still good. I ain't gon' let nothing happen to you—"

"Well, why you take my muthafuckin' strap, nigga?!" I yelled at him with my jaw clenched tight.

"Yeah, man, that's some fuck shit!" Lil Willy chimed in, looking at G.

"'Cause, nigga, I'm tryna keep it one hundred wit'cha. A lot of niggaz getting ready to get slumped, and I don't want my Auntie Carol making no more funeral arrangements."

G was talking about my mother. The last funeral my mama went to was for one of her boyfriends, Jeff, and G was a suspect in that murder investigation. The two didn't get along. He was gunned down on his front steps at his mama's house.

"Man, what the fuck is you talking about? Gimme back my shit, and I'll holla at y'all niggas later." He was trying me, just like we used to do sucka ass niggas, and I wasn't feeling it.

"Is you fucking with dat bitch Kadisha?" G asked.

I hesitated because I knew that everything with him was

always carefully planned and orchestrated for his next move.

"Nawl, I ain't fucking with her no more. Why?" I asked.

For the first time, a sign of relief showed on G's face. "'Cause that bitch is history. Right now, as we speak, my nigga Steve is getting ready to gun smoke dat hoe. She wanna play pussy, she finna get fucked."

CHAPTER
Twenty-Two

Mellow

"Whaat?!" my voice screeched. I was heated. I took a step toward G with a scowl on my face.

"Nigga, don't you go catchin' feelings for no bitch. That hoe ain't shit. We ran up in that bitch crib on some home invasion shit. I fucked that hoe and muted her fuck ass. She scratched my face. I woulda killed the bitch, but she played dead after I shot her in the head. Lucky she didn't see my face, or I'd be in jail now."

G was wrong. Kadisha had seen his face.

It took everything in my power to control my emotions when I tried to reason with G. With sympathy in my voice, I said, "G, come on, dog. That girl is only seventeen years old. She lost her family and err'thang she loved. Now you wanna kill her. For what, man?"

"My nigga, it's bigger than me and you. It was all part of the plan from day one. She gotta die. Her little brother in the hospital has to die, too. My niggaz working on that as we speak. And when and if that fuck nigga Big Bee gets out of jail, his ass gon' get murked, too."

E-Class sniggered and blew that stinking ass smoke in my direction. Then he coughed like he was about to go into a seizure. A big ass cockroach scurried across the table and dived onto his lap. Somebody chuckled. It felt like my heart was hemorrhaging. I was hurting. I didn't realize my feelings for Kadisha were so strong. Strong enough to make me want to kill my own blood for her.

"Come on, man. You taking this shit too far. Y'all niggaz eating good, getting plenty of paper, and making millions. Dog, she's only seventeen years old!"

"I can't unring the bell once it has been rung," G commented in a fog of smoke.

"Yes, you can!" I had steel in my voice, and for the first time in my life, I would have fought G, even killed him.

Then, something else occurred to me, and I vented. "And on top of that, you fuckin' wit that slimy ass nigga Steve! Call it off, man," I pleaded, suddenly looking for an exit from the crowded room.

"Steve? Dat nigga loyal as fuck. He told me about the sucka-for-love ass shit you did in front of Kadisha that day we ran up in there. If you had fucked that lick up, I was going to come looking for you, and it wouldn't have been nice. From day one, Steve was the inside man who set the lick up!"

"That nigga ain't shit. He set my nigga Bell up, took his money, and got him whacked."

"That was my work. I set up Bell and got him whacked. He was Rah-Rah's nephew. That nigga is two bodies up on me. You ain't seen shit yet. I know where Rah-Rah's momma lives now," G bragged.

My legs turned to jelly. It was like I was standing in front of a speeding Mack truck and couldn't get out of the way. Absentmindedly, I reached for my phone in my pocket to send Kadisha a text. I had accidentally left the phone in my car.

"Fuck!"

"Man, y'all niggaz on some bullshit." Lil Willy scoffed, looking around.

"Your lil' ass gon' be out there in dat muthufuckin' dumpster if you keep talkin' slick," E-Class said as he passed the blunt to K-9 and busted open another blunt. He prepared to build it with his cocktail of Molly, coke, and weed. We called it Bunk.

Suddenly, my emotions got the best of me. I had to get to Kadisha; I had to save her. I needed to get out of that cramped kitchen, away from G and his goons. There was no doubt whatsoever what I would have to do.

I HAD the Glock 16-shot nine-millimeter in the small of my back, tucked in my pants. I could see G's hands; they were empty. However, I knew he had a pistol in his pants. *Altogether, there are eight of us in this room,* I thought as my pulse raced. My nerves quaked as my heart thumped.

It was about to be on!

"So, what you want from me? Cause I'm finna bail," I said and glanced over at Lil Willy, secretly giving him the signal to get ready. I knew he still had the nine that he had shown me earlier.

"What I want from you is that muthufuckin' safe that was in Kadisha's house that her daddy had stashed," G said, walking up and chest-bumping me. He used to do the exact same thing when we were shorties, right before he whipped my ass. He was about two inches taller than me.

"Man, I don't know what the fuck you're talkin' about." I stood my ground.

"I feel like you down with that bitch, Kadisha, na'mean. I keep telling you that hoe ain't shit. Don't play with me, Mell. I'll bust that ass. You know how I get down."

"Man, like I said, I don't know what you're talkin' 'bout!" I didn't budge an inch the entire time. I was thinking about pulling out. He was my own flesh and blood, but I didn't have a choice. It was him or me.

"Okay... okay...." G took a step away and glowered. I could tell his mind was deep in thought. He was considering something—a different approach, a different method, or maybe a quick way to dispose of us. Then he dropped another bomb on me.

"Since you're here, I might as well let you know the latest update on the John Doe Boys' territories take over, just in case you didn't get the hood memo, nigga." G sneered with them fake ass ivory teeth he paid ten stacks for. "From Carol City, Opa-Locka, Hialeah, The Grove, The Pork and Beans Projects, none of y'all niggaz can sell dope no more unless it's my dope, na'mean, and I approve it."

"Ahh, fuck nawl!" Lil Willy grumbled under his breath. I noticed his hand inching for his strap. Mine was doing the same...

It was about to be some gunplay.

It suddenly hit me like a ton of bricks; this had been one of G's ploys from day one. To get me here and try to bleed me for information about Kadisha's daddy's safe and try to bitch me up and take my trap.

"I ain't gon' be able to let you do it," I said and caught Lil Willy's eye, a warning to get ready.

At that point, it was obvious that there was a chance we wouldn't walk out of there alive.

"You ain't gon' be able to let me do what, nigga?" G asked with a knotted brow.

"I ain't gon' be able to let you take my trap, nigga!" The room erupted in harsh talking. G's clique wanted to bring the pain, slaughter us right there in the kitchen, and get it over with.

"Y'all niggaz might not even walk out of here alive, fo-reel fo-reel," E-Class said and flicked a roach off his pants.

"Nigga, I'll beat your fuckin' ass," G said, enraged. He placed his hand in my face like he was going to steal on me.

I must have struck a nerve. "G, I ain't no shawty no-mo. You might whip my ass, but I'm fighting back and dats on err'thang," I said, dead-ass-serious.

The entire time, I replayed in my mind, like a video game, just who I was going to shoot first. I decided it was G —he was the immediate threat. Bam was leaning against the refrigerator; he would be next because he was toting the 'stick.' Then I'd shoot the two other dudes who were standing by the stove. They didn't appear to be strapped, but I was about to find out.

"I see you smelling yourself, little nigga. You're eighteen now and think just cause you blood, you can't get it too. Well, you're wrong." G looked over at K-9, one of the dudes with the 'stick' and said, "Yo, y'all take these niggas out back to the dumpster and dispose of their asses like trash—" G was midsentence when suddenly, there was a loud knock on the front door. G looked away from me toward the door.

The lookout scout shouted with panic in his voice, "Rah-Rah and 'em just came through here in an old Buick LeSabre, full of niggas!"

G turned, damn near jumping two feet off the floor, and started issuing orders to his crew. Obviously, Rah-Rah didn't have a problem coming through on a kamikaze suicide mission to air that bitch out.

"Everybody on deck! Don't let them niggas off the block this time!" G yelled above the clamor of noise.

E-Class stood from the table, damn near knocking it over with his big, blubber belly. He was surprisingly quick for a big dude. Lil Willy and I exchanged knowing glances at the same time amid the confusion.

It was either now or never.

Then it happened. Lil Willy was the smallest man in the room with the biggest heart. He drew his banger and shot E-Class in the back of the head, causing blood to splatter. Brain matter sprayed the room in a misty haze as the big man flipped, crashing over the table.

Then, all hell broke loose!

G turned back around and looked at me. It was as if time stopped. The moment stalled, moving in slow, surreal motion. Lil Willy continued busting his gun. Shots were returned; it was pure chaos. G and I were standing too close in proximity. There wasn't enough room, not enough space. Some of G's dudes returned fire as they ran out the door for cover. G reached for his strap just as I reached for mine.

I was too slow.

At point-blank range, he aimed for my head as gunshots erupted around us like we were in a battle zone.

Boom! Boom! Blocka! Blocka! Ka-Boom! Ka-Boom!

The shots rang out from all kinds of high-powered weapons and an assortment of handguns.

CHAPTER
Twenty-Three

Mellow

I felt a surge of heat hit me in my arm, slightly staggering me. Bullets whistled past my head as I realized I'd been shot. I returned fire. I'll never forget seeing the look on G's face as he fell backward, firing at me aimlessly in blind rage. His Gucci shirt was stained with blood and puffed up twice with each bullet I dumped into his body as he collapsed on the floor. I'd hit him in the chest with my nine.

'I shot my own flesh and blood.'

'I possibly killed him.'

'I was defending myself.'

Those were the dreary thoughts that flashed through my mind. Then, disturbingly, it occurred to me that I should have finished him off, but I didn't because I couldn't. Instead, operating on instincts and adrenalin, I rushed on.

The gunshots continued to blast a deafening sound. I turned around blindly as the gun battle continued. With my eyes closed, blinking sporadically, I randomly fired a few more shots at the two dudes with the sticks. One of the gunmen had me locked in his sights. AK-47 aimed at my head, he fired. The gun clicked. The weapon was either out of bullets, or it jammed. In an instant, the side of his face exploded. Lil Willy had shot him in the face. He was taking full advantage of his small size, evasive like crack smoke. He was hard to shoot.

. Or so I thought...

In all the commotion, I turned and looked at Willy. He had been hit, too, in the chest, but he was still shooting the big gun like he was unfazed. Maybe it was from all the 'lean' that he had been drinking, but he bounced on his feet, hyperactive and animated, shooting as if he was throwing bullets from his gun. The entire right side of his shirt was red. I remember thinking this was inhuman and unreal. We needed to make an exit from the apartment. Virtually all of G's men had made a mad dash for the door.

"Willy! Come on!" I yelled, stepping over my cousin G as he struggled. He was reaching for the gat under the table like a dying man, determined to go out with dignity but doomed.

Lil Willy kicked the gun away and aimed at G's head.

"No!" I hollered.

Lil Willy stopped. There were three bodies cluttering

the room, along with the horrid smell of blood, latent gun smoke, and death.

"Man, if you don't kill dis fuck nigga, he gon' come back and kill us," Lil Willy said with blood streaming from his shirt.

"Okay, kill 'em."

"No!" G screamed like bitch, flailing his arms to ward off the shot.

Then we both heard it at the same time: bloodcurdling screams and the sound of an assault weapon that roared like hell on earth. I had never heard anything like it before.

"Wha-da-fuck?!"

Then, a body came crashing through the door, riddled with bullets. The head was partially severed, guts open and spewing out.

Lil Willy thought he shot G. We exited the kitchen. Both of us were leaking badly.

Big mistake leaving G alive...

WE RAN into the living room into an ambush. The black woman who owned the apartment was screaming at the top of her lungs. There were bodies on top of bodies piled at the door while the sound of thunderous gunfire continued to erupt. The front door was open, which was where the shots were coming from.

Then, somebody yelled, "The po-po coming up the block!"

With no other recourse and nothing to lose, we ran toward the front door and were instantly confronted by two masked gunmen. One held an old Thompson machine gun with a specially-altered hundred-round drum clip that was built to wreak havoc and slaughter everything in its way, and it did! Bullets spit from it at rapid fire, nonstop, at ten rounds per second.

We were trapped, doomed like sitting ducks. I aimed my gun to fire... too slow. My arm was mangled from a gunshot wound. Lil Willy was behind me. He never saw death staring us in the face as the smoldering gray gun smoke bellowed, enveloping us.

Then, the strangest thing happened. The gunman hesitated as someone continued to shout, "The po-po coming! Let's go! Let's go!"

The gunman pulled up the mask and furrowed his brow into a tight line across his face. He had a crazed, manic look in his eyes.

"My nigga, what the fuck y'all doin here?! Where dat fuck nigga G at?"

It was Rah-Rah with an illegal ass Thompson Submachine gun. It wasn't even fair the way he had been plowing down niggaz like a lawn mower cutting grass. The hall was littered with bodies, dudes moaning in agony.

Lil Willy peeked from behind me, prepared to shoot, but I shoved his gun.

Rah-Rah groaned, "Aww, man."

Lil Willy was in bad condition by then. The 'lean' was wearing off. Him and Rah-Rah were tight. Lil Willy was his dude. Rah-Rah shoved me and Lil Willy out of the way, prepared to enter the apartment in search of G. The other masked gunman stood with an AR-15 aimed at my chest.

Just as Rah-Rah was about to push past us, a voice shouted from down the hall.

"Police, FREEZE right there!"

Rah-Rah turned and let loose with the submachine gun. He sprayed the hall, knocking big chunks out of the cinder block as brick and debris fell from the walls. It looked like we were trapped in a violent tornado. The cop dropped. His partner returned fire and was instantly killed, too.

Lil Willy and I took off running down the hall in one direction and Rah-Rah and his dude in the other.

As we approached the landing of the steps, Lil Willy fell. His gun fell down the stairs, as his eyes started rolling. A trickle of blood poured from his mouth as he tried to tell me something.

"Come on, man! Come on, my nigga! Get up!"

At that moment, I heard the sirens. The police were coming. I reached down and picked Lil Willy up. Pain ricocheted through my body. I turned to move down the stairs and out of the building. I noticed a little girl with pink barrettes and sad eyes brimming with tears watching us as she held her little brother's hand. He was about five years old with a snotty nose and dirty clothes. Lil Willy's gun was next to the boy's feet as they stood in the pissy smelling stairwell looking at us. This would probably not be their last time witnessing such a horrific gun battle. This was a way of life.

As SOON as we exited the project building, herds of people stood around gawking. I was practically dragging Lil Willy.

"Ahhh, shit. Ahhh shit, look at them," Voices droned as we walked.

The crowd opened, making a path for us. We made it to my car, leaving behind a trail of blood, suspense, and deadly drama.

As soon as I started the engine, a cop car came speeding right for us, then came to a screeching stop as it reached my car. The cops hopped out with their guns drawn and ran into the building we had just exited. Not even a second later, a caravan of cop cars came swarming into the projects.

I drove off, slow and calm, hoping like a muthafucka we didn't get pulled over. The entire time, I could hear Lil Willy mumbling inaudibly as he grimaced in pain.

"My nigga, you straight?" I asked, looking into the

review mirror as I turned on 27th. It was a long stretch of street, perfect to blend in with the traffic.

"Fuck nawl, I ain't straight..." Lil Willy groaned and picked up his cup of lean off the floorboard.

"I'ma take you to the hospital," I said as I sped down the street.

I just happened to glance down at the seat. My phone was flashing, letting me know I had missed a phone call or a text. I picked up and, again, winced in pain. There was a text from Kadisha. I tried to manipulate the phone with one hand and steer with the other, but the phone was slippery with blood.

"Man, I'm getting cold... Man... I think I'm finna die... man." That was my first time ever hearing fear in Lil Willy's voice.

"You gon' make it, man. I got you. We headed to the hospital now."

"I'm not gon' make it."

"Nigga, shut up!" I said, looking in his direction with the phone in my hand.

Silence.

I was finally able to get a grip on the phone as I ran a light at a busy intersection, headed for Miami Memorial Hospital. I managed to read the text.

Mell, help. Come get me. I'm at

"Fuck! Shit!" I banged my hand on the steering wheel. Lil Willy flinched, and his eyes popped wide open.

"Nigga, slow down. You driving too damn fast! Where you going?"

"I'm taking you to the hospital—"

"Nigga, I ain't goin' ta no fuckin' hospital. I got a warrant for violation of probation. They gon' take me to jail."

"Which one do you prefer? To go to jail or hell?"

"Man, I ain't goin' ta no fucking hell. You got mo bodies than me."

Vaguely, I could hear what he was rumbling about, but my mind was elsewhere. Yeah, I had been shot, but my wound was not as serious as his. There was an exit wound in the back of my shoulder. The bullet had gone in and come out. Other than extreme pain, I was okay. At least the blood had stopped running from my arm, which was not the case for Lil Willy.

By the time I pulled up to the hospital, Lil Willy was deliriously talking to himself, mumbling on and on. When we entered the hospital emergency room, it was already crowded with people. Two armed guards stood at the nurses' station. One of them was a cop. As soon as he saw us, all bloody and haggard like we had just left a war zone, he got on his radio.

I placed Willy in a wheelchair by the door. As soon as the blond-haired nurse sitting at the desk saw us, she took off running along with a male nurse. He may have been a doctor because he was dressed in green scrubs and had a surgical mask on his head. The two cops rushed over as well. We had started a commotion; one of the cops was an obese white dude with sagging chins and gaunt eyes. He came and stood directly behind me like he was guarding the door.

"We're going to need a stretcher and prepare for immediate surgery," the guy in the scrubs said.

I eased away, walking backward. As I turned to leave, the fat guard yelled, "Heyy, you! Stop! Where you going?"

I ran out the hospital door, almost knocking over an elderly lady and a man with a walking cane. I ran and hopped into my Chevy. The night sky was dotted with luminous helicopter lights, searching. I mashed out just as cop cars turned into the hospital parking lot, followed by a stream of ambulances. At that time, I didn't know my cousin G was in one of them. Somehow, he had survived.

I bent a corner and got on the expressway. I just drove, destination unknown, with my thoughts whirling as I wracked my brain. Where in the fuck was Kadisha? I felt a sharp pain in my shoulder. I didn't know what caliber pistol I was hit with, but that bitch hurt like fuck.

In the cup holder was Lil Willy's drink, a half cup of lean, dark purple. The darker the drink, the more potent and expensive. There was probably three hundred dollars' worth of lean in the cup. I turned the cup up, and the sweet juice dribbled down my chin. Moments later, the pleasant euphoria of the high hit me, causing the pain in my arm to go away.

I strained my brain and started thinking deep thoughts. *Why did G want Kadisha's entire family dead? Who else was behind it? G said it was bigger than him. Maybe Kadisha's father owed some Colombians money. Maybe it was Kadisha's trifling ass aunt or her mother.* Then, something dawned on me. It was something G said when we first pulled up at his spot, and they drew down on us. He was talking to Tat-Tat. He had told him and Mike Dee to go to the Lafayette Motel.

Could that possibly be where Kadisha was meeting Steve? I didn't know. But one thing was certain: I had to find her.

I had to.

CHAPTER
Twenty-Four

Kadisha

I drove the Dodge Charger with the top down, the wind in my face, and my mind on the moment as the souped-up engine purred like a deadly melody. The Miami nightlife welcomed me, alive and enchanting like the thoughts that barged their way into my head, into my heart. For some reason, anger continued to consume me. I thought about my little brother in that hospital bed, so delicate, so fragile. It was hard for me to imagine that Steve, of all people, was responsible for it, along with the deaths of my little sister, Ms. Shay, and possibly my dad. I couldn't take it any longer. I pulled the car over into a Shell gas station and dialed Steve's number.

"Yo, what it do, ma?" he answered.

"What hotel you want me to meet you at?" I tersely asked.

Steve must have sensed something because he asked, "You aight? Sounds like something wrong wit'cha."

I softened my tone and glanced at my reflection in the rearview mirror just as a group of cute dudes pulled up and got out of a nice white Tahoe with big rims and a banging sound system. As they walked toward my car in the gas station, they glanced at me for a moment and frowned, like they were looking at someone from another planet. Then they looked away. I had gauze wrapped around my head and no lip gloss. I must have looked a hot mess. I wasn't used to that. Dudes always tried to holla at me. I frowned at my reflection and began to yank at the gauze wrapped around my head as I talked to Steve.

"Yeah... I'm ready... what hotel you get a room at, boo?" I said in a fake voice.

"I'm at the Lafayette. We gon' get turned up. I got a bottle of Cîroc and some good weed. I'ma lick that pussy like you like it. You still gon' let me hit that ass, right?"

"Aww, yeah. I'm going to let you hit this, and you can have all the pussy you want. In fact, I want you to do me a favor," I said with tears in my voice as I continued to unwrap the gauze while staring at my shaved skull and the grisly scar on the side of my head. I looked like something out of a horror movie.

"What you want me to teach you? It better be something freaky."

"It is. I want you to teach me how to suck dick and swallow your cum. Can you do that for me, Steve?" I said and wiped at the tear running down my cheek. Then I patted my long hair over the scar, thinking about how I used to be a beautiful girl. As best as I could, I tried to conceal the ugly, pinkish scar.

"Hell yeah!! I'ma show you how to suck dick and shallow. That's what the fuck I'm talking about!" he exhorted excitedly. "Come to room one ten. It's in the back. Don't wear any panties."

"Okay. I'm on my way now," I said as I smoothed my hair and disconnected the call.

I applied pink lip balm and puckered my lips in the mirror. The blow torch was on the passenger's seat. I looked over at it, imagining what I was going to do to Steve's dick. I was going to burn his ass, and it wouldn't be with no STD.

The cute guys who had entered the gas station's store walked out with cases of beer. One of the dudes had dark skin, a handsome face, and pretty teeth. He had dimples and a dazzling smile when he spoke. "What's up, shawty?"

"Damn! Where the hell you come from?" his friend chimed in.

"If you ain't got a boyfriend, lemme get them digits."

His partner was a cutie. He had a pecan complexion with a Miami Heat cap and a crisp white t-shirt. He shoved his friend and stepped to me.

"She don't date boyfriends. She dates men like me. Ain't that right, sexy?"

He made a comical face, and they all laughed as they flirted with me. Despite my discontentment, a smile tugged at my cheeks, then died when I thought about Steve and what I was about to do to him. I placed the car in gear and drove off.

I decided against going to my house to change clothes and take a shower. It was as if I was possessed by something uncontrollable, the undeniable will to kill. Maybe it was because of that first shot I fired into dude's head at Mellow's house. It had done something to me that was irreversible. There was no turning back now. My first taste of revenge was sweet, and I relished it. Maybe if I hadn't experienced so much death and violence in my life at such a young age, things would have been different.

I PULLED into the hotel parking lot located in a rundown section of town. The parking lot was full of tricked-out cars. The location was a haven for hustlers and hoes. I scanned the room doors, looking for the number Steve had given me. I found it all the way around back. Steve's Camry was parked out front. I parked several cars down with the bumper against the wall, just as my dad would always do when we went to a hotel. For the first time, I understood why: to make it hard for anyone to read the tag number. I was starting to think like a gangsta's daughter.

For a moment, I sat idle, watching the room door as I gathered my thoughts. I exhaled a deep breath of courage, prepared to do what I had to do. Even if it meant serving life in prison, I was going to do it. I took the gun out of my purse and held it. Again, I felt a surge of energy. The kind of energy that only power brings when you're getting ready to seek revenge. I checked my reflection in the mirror. Then, remembering Steve's request, I undressed, taking my bra and panties off. I shoved them in my purse. Then, I continued to hold the gun.

As I put the convertible top up, preparing to get out, my phone chimed, startling me. I looked at the caller ID just as a cop car pulled into the parking lot, doing a slow creep. I remained as still as a mannequin with the gun in my hand. For some reason, I was holding my breath as I clutched the gun in one hand and my phone in the other as it continued to ring. The cop pulled right next to me and glanced into the car. I must have looked suspicious, sitting in a nice car in a high-crime area that was known for prostitution and drugs.

The cop got out of the car and walked over to my car.

"Oh, God," I groaned and dropped the gun on the floorboard.

It was Sergeant Malcolm Steel, the cop who was investigating my family's case. He had changed clothes from earlier and now wore a sky-blue Polo shirt, blue jeans, and black Nike sneakers. For some reason, I stared at the Glock holstered at his side as he tapped on my window. I hesitated and let it down.

He raised his brow. "Kadisha?"

He then bent down and looked inside the car, then at my breasts that were damn near fully exposed with the top buttons of my blouse undone.

"What are you doing here? This is a bad area of town to be in."

"I... I'm here to pick up a friend."

"Hmm, well, you need to be careful. I'm not supposed to tell you this, but we have reason to believe that your family tragedy may have been a contract hit, and your life may be in danger." As he talked, he continued to scan the parking lot.

I pretended to be shocked, which wasn't hard to do. I placed my hand over my heart, trying to furtively cover the exposed cleavage.

"Oh, my God! Are you serious?"

"Yes, I'm serious. You may need to leave town until we find the culprits."

"Okay, I was going to medical school in the fall, anyway," I lied.

He nodded his head, but I could tell his mind was churning; he was thinking in police mode. He just looked at me, then stepped back and made a mental note of the car.

"Judging from the information we have as it relates to suspects, the people who invaded your family's home may have also been in search of something. We know there were drugs and money, but there was something else. Do you have any idea what it could be?" he asked.

I played dumb. I knew it was my father's safe, but I pretended to ponder my thoughts. At that moment, a prostitute walked out of a room with an old, white trick. The man had a large belly and was slightly stooped over from age. He looked to be in his late sixties with balding, gray hair as he shook his finger at the prostitute.

"Heyyy, you just gon' take my money?"

"Ta-ta, love. I told you five hundred dollars for an hour of my time. It ain't my fault you couldn't get it up," the prostitute caroled in a sing-song voice as if taunting the old dude.

She had on a long, blond wig and a black miniskirt that was so short I could see her booty cheeks when she walked in her six-inch heels. She looked to be around my age.

I looked away from the prostitute and responded, "No, I don't know what they could have been searching for."

Sergeant Steel just looked at me, and then he looked over at the prostitute as she passed, calling him by his name. He spoke and then turned back to me. His words caught me by surprise.

"I hope you don't get into any trouble. I know you were raised in the Pork and Bean projects, and you came up impoverished, the daughter of a gangster, but now you're a college graduate and are about to make something of your life. These streets will eat you up and spit you out. You'll be just like that girl you just saw with the white guy. She's twenty years old, and this is her life. I don't want to see you around here no more. Is that understood?" He gave me a quick once over again, glancing at my semi-exposed breasts. He may have thought I was there whoring. One thing was certain. He knew I was up to something.

I gave him a subtle nod and watched as he turned and walked off.

Sergeant Malcolm Steel was about to be the thorn in my side. He would be one of my biggest problems when the drama popped off. I should have taken my butt home that day, but I didn't.

I expelled a deep sigh as he walked away. My phone continued to ring. I answered, and it was my girl, Shamika.

"Bitch, you didn't have to tell us you wasn't going back home," she blasted me.

I could hear Latoya in the background, putting her two cents in. "Yeah, hoe, you didn't have to tell us."

"Bitch, all you had to do was call and ask," I said with an overwhelming feeling of relief.

Shamika and Latoya were my real homegirls. We were tight, and I was so happy to hear from them that I didn't know what to do. I just smiled as I watched the patrol car leave the parking lot.

"Where you at, girl?" Shamika asked.

"If I told you, you wouldn't believe me."

"Try, bitch! Your ass probably laid up somewhere with fine ass Mellow playing with your coochie."

For some reason, I giggled. I heard Latoya laughing in the background.

"Nawl, girl, I wish. I'm sitting in the parking lot at the Lafayette, about to do something I might regret, but I've come too far already to turn back."

"What you talkin' 'bout, bitch? Sounding all sad 'n shit... And what the fuck you got going on? You don't have your girls with you!"

"I found out who was involved in the home invasion—"

"You lying! Ohh, uhh, noo, girl. Get the fuck outta here! Who? Did you tell the police?" Shamika screamed over the phone.

"Hell, nawl. My daddy didn't raise me to be no damn snitch. Besides, this is personal."

"Who did it? Come on, tell me, hoe. Stop playing! You better not do shit without your girls!" I could imagine hyperactive ass Shamika jumping up and down.

Then, the hotel curtain moved. I saw Steve standing in the window, watching me sit in the car. My heart did a somersault. I suddenly felt an adrenaline rush.

"I'll tell you later. Just let me handle this business first," I said and hung up the phone.

HESITANTLY, I knocked on the door. I looked around nervously as I tried my best to shake the jitters. Suddenly, I remembered something and unbuttoned my blouse all the way down to the second from the last button, exposing a lot of cleavage. My small, perky breasts were basically visible.

The door opened a crack, and Steve peered out. I smiled at him and thrust my chest forward, making my titties jiggle.

I felt a pang in my stomach and a lot of nervous energy as I said in a jovial tone, "Open the door, boy. Let me come in." I smiled.

Steve stared at me with glassy eyes. There was something wrong with his demeanor. Finally, he opened the door and let me in.

It was on!

CHAPTER
Twenty-Five

Kadisha

I walked inside and instantly recognized the awful smell. Steve was smoking primos, which is a cigarette laced with powder cocaine. I had always suspected that he was on drugs, but now I knew for sure.

Steve shut the door, wearing only a wife beater and True Religion jeans. He had something stashed behind his hand as he looked at me. There was music playing from a CD player on the dresser.

Something was wrong. This was not what I expected. The hotel room was cluttered with beer cans and open cigar packages from rolling blunts. Clothes and shoes were thrown about as well. There was a pile of cocaine on a table and some small, clear baggies, along with a wad of cash. Steve must have had this hotel room all along; he had been trapping out of it. That explained why he had me come to a hotel in the heart of the ghetto.

"Who did you tell you were coming here?" he asked and peered out the window.

Steve then turned around and looked me up and down. He stared at my breasts as he massaged his dick through his pants. Like he was in some type of perpetual paranoia, he looked out the window again. He turned back toward me, unzipped his pants, and started stroking himself. That's when I saw the gun at his side. A sheen of perspiration gleamed on his forehead, and his eyes bulged like he was geeking. High from smoking too much coke and paranoid.

I pretended like I didn't see the gun or notice him geeking and strolled over to the bed.

"Boy, don't get me all the way over here and chicken out on me. You told me you was going to eat my stuff," I said with a fake laugh as it dawned on me that Steve had other intentions. Aside from having sex with me, he was up to something else. I was certain of it.

But what?

"In time, but I need to know where your daddy's safe at."

"What-da-fuck?!" I blurted out.

I couldn't help it. This nigga wasn't even trying to sugar-coat it. He was behind my family's tragedy and my daddy's disappearance. I had to control myself, though. I needed to place his mind at ease and then rock his ass to sleep for eternity!

"I mean, what are you talking about, Steve?" I said in a mild voice and tried to smile, but my cheeks refused.

"It's just that I've given your father some personal items, and I need them shits back." He glanced out the curtain again as he continued to stroke himself.

It took everything in my power not to roll my eyes. I had to be careful; he was geeking with a gun in his hand, which made him even more dangerous.

"I don't know what happened to that safe, but that ain't what I came all the way here for," I said and took off my blouse.

He stared at my titties, then said, "What you holding that purse for? Take the rest of them clothes off."

"What you holding that gun for?" I retorted and smiled generically.

He didn't answer. That wasn't a good sign; I needed to place his mind at ease. I tossed the purse on the table by the bed and almost knocked over a bottle of Hennessy.

One thing that always captivated him, even back in high school, was to see me dance and shake my big ass.

I strolled over to the CD player on the dresser and turned the volume up. "Tapout" by Lil Wayne, Nicki Minaj, and Future was playing. Nicki sang melodiously. "Eat this pussy, this pussy. I got the world's best pussy.

I began to gyrate my hips, humping the air as I let my skirt fall from my body. Completely nude, I turned around and jiggled my ass, then made it clap. As the bass rhythm of the song played, I began to twerk to the beat, bouncing up and down, and then I bent all the way over, making both cheeks bounce separately. That was a trick I'd learned from watching chicks on YouTube. All Steve could see with me bent over was a bald ass pussy and my big ole booty.

"Goddamnmuthufucka!" he droned like he was in a hypnotic and stroked himself faster. Then he dropped his pants. His dick was hard, sticking straight up in his boxer shorts as he walked over and grinded his dick against me.

"I'ma fuck the shit outta you," he groaned lustfully.

I turned around and danced close up on him. "Ahh, huh, but first you gotta eat this pussy like you said," I cajoled in a sexy voice. "Then you gon' teach me how to suck that dick, right?" I teased him.

Still dancing, I placed my finger in his mouth. He licked on my finger like I was something sweet to eat, then said in a strained voice, "Get on the bed. Let a nigga sample that fat ass pussy like a gourmet meal. We finna do some real freaky shit." He placed the gun on the nightstand by the bed.

Got him! I thought, but I needed my purse with the gun in it.

"Let me use the bathroom and freshen up. I'll be right back," I said while I danced.

I was rocking my hips and pressing my pelvis against his dick as I caressed his balls. My purse was only a few feet away, next to the bed. Just as I reached for it, he grabbed my arm in a vise grip.

"Wuz up with you and that purse? What you got in there?" He moved toward the purse to look inside.

If he found the gun, it would be over for me. I had to do something quick!

I snatched his boxer shorts and heard them rip when I pulled him back toward me and dropped to my knees.

"I thought you said you were going to teach me how to suck dick," I said, looking up at him. I placed my mouth over the bulge and breathed my hot breath. Then I began to kiss on the head of his dick.

"Ahhhh, sh... sh... sheeeiit!" he droned and grabbed the back of my head, pressing my face down on his dick. Then he whipped it out and tried to force me to suck it. The entire time, I stared at my purse with the gun in it.

"Just put it into your mouth, suck it, and watch your teeth," he persuaded aggressively.

This was not the Steve I knew—the guy I thought I had wrapped around my pinkie. Something about him frightened me. I honestly felt he would kill me. So, I thought about my family and the tragedy he had caused as I stared at my purse on the table. Then, I pinched my eyes closed and let him humiliate me and abuse me, but in the back of my mind, I knew I had to get my hands on that gun.

I took his dick into my mouth and began to suck on it as best I could.

Ugh!

I gagged and almost vomited twice as he shoved his long, skinny dick down my throat. I had never felt so humiliated in my life, on my knees, with his dick in my mouth, in a dirty, cheap, hotel room.

God help me.

"Come on, girl. Suck the dick! Suck it harder!" He grabbed my face with both hands and started humping my mouth.

Just that fast, the tables had turned. It became obvious that Steve had every intention of dogging me out. There was nothing romantic about this encounter. Instinctively, I knew that depending on how I acted, I could make the situation worse. I couldn't help but wonder if he had another agenda... plans that involved more than just sexing me.

Instantly, my mind flashed back to what Mellow had warned me, *"You could be walking into a trap. Steve could be trying to set you up."*

I gagged, choked, and spit his dick out. Looking up at him, I said, "Let's lay down. My knees are hurting."

Steve just stared down at me as sweat poured from his face. He had a fiendish scowl that hinted at a smile. Then, he began to masturbate. His body made a jerky motion, and it suddenly dawned on me what he was doing. He wanted to cum on my face.

I think not!

I stood and strode over to the bed, sashaying my ass from side to side. My purse was only a few inches away, within arm's reach. I looked over my shoulder. Steve was right behind me with his long dick stabbing me in my back.

I lay down on my back, mentally measuring the distance between me and my purse as he eased his sweaty body on top of me. With his head between my legs, he spread my vagina lips, using a forefinger and his tongue, and began to lick, lapping at my pussy.

"Ohhhh, yess, yess," I pretended to moan as I grinded my pussy in his face, leaning over, reaching... reaching... for my purse on the table. Just as I was about to grab it, Steve came up for air, nearly catching me. His lips were shiny with my juices.

I smiled like I was in heaven and asked, "What's wrong, baby?"

"I want you to do me a favor," he said with a pained expression.

"Yeah, sure. What is it?" I softly asked.

"I want you to stick your finger in my ass while I jack off."

"Whaat?!" I screeched, sitting up on my elbows and looking at his crazy ass.

Hell-to-the-mufuckin-nawl. This nigga was taking this shit too far. I didn't sign up for this shit. I wasn't a sex expert, but what he said sounded homosexual to me.

Just as I was about to protest, I realized he would have to turn his back for me to stick my finger up his nasty ass. Then, I could get to the gun.

"Yeah, sure," I said with a straight face and watched as he grabbed the primo cigarette from the ashtray and fired it up. He licked it because it was burning sideways. His eyes grew big as he sucked on the cocaine-laced cigarette.

Then, he cocked his head to the side and whispered, "You hear dat?"

231

"Hear what?" I whispered back. This was my first time seeing him high and paranoid.

"Shhhh!" he hissed for me to be quiet, throwing up his hand.

We sat like that for damn near twenty minutes. With his head cocked to the side like a baby bird waiting to be fed, he listened to imaginary noises. Steve was buggin' out.

He took a long drink from the bottle of Hennessey, frowned, and whispered, "You ready?

"Ready for what?"

"To stick your finger up my ass."

All I could do was nod my head like a deaf mute. I was afraid to trust my voice to speak as I watched him spit on his hand and wipe it in the crack of his butt. He flipped onto his stomach, tooted his booty up, and began to masturbate.

"Come on, hurry up," he urged.

"Okay, here I come," I said as I reached inside the purse and grabbed the gun.

"Damn, your finger feels cold," Steve wiggled his ass and complained while jacking his dick, barely on his knees with his face in the pillow.

"That's because it's a nine-millimeter up in your ass. Now, tell me where my father is before I pull the trigger."

"Oh, shit!" he grumbled.

CHAPTER
Twenty-Six

Kadisha

With a pillowcase over his head, I was able to tie each of Steve's arms and legs to the bedpost, spread eagle, with the electrical cord from the CD player.

"I can't believe you, of all people, set up my father and was responsible for all the killings and bloodshed."

"Wh... What are you talking 'bout, girl? Stop playin' and take this pillowcase and fuckin' cord off me. I didn't have nothing to do with that shit." Steve thrashed, trying to get loose from the restraints.

"Oh, I'm not playing, and I'm getting ready to show you. Now, tell me where my father is," I said as I tried to light the blow torch with a Bic lighter.

"I don't know what you're talking about!" he yelled, raising his head off the bed with the pillowcase over it.

Phoof! The blow torch finally lit. He flinched.

"What was dat?" He thrashed his neck from side to side.

"That was the sound of the lie detector test I'm getting ready to submit you to," I said in a clipped tone as I stared at the small blue flame.

"Girl, stop it! I don't know what the hell you're talking about. I had nothing to do with your family's murder or your dad's disappearance. Mellow did it."

"Oh, yeah? Then tell me who Michael Thomson is." That was the guy who I shot in the head after he confessed that G and Steve were behind the murders of my family.

"I... I... I don't know what you're talking about. I didn't have nothing to do with that shit!"

"Wrong answer!"

I pressed the blow torch to his inner thigh next to his balls. There was a sizzling sound of burning flesh as Steve howled in agony. Instantly, the room filled with the awful scent of burning flesh.

"Ohh, God! Ohh, God! Stop it! Pah-leees stop it!!"

I removed the torch from his leg. There was a deep, ugly gash smoldering. Steve panted, struggling to breathe as I spoke.

"Where is my father? You better tell me, or I'm going to burn your ass again."

"I swear to God I had nothin' ta do with—"

I pressed the torch to his thigh and watched him thrash like he was being electrocuted by a million watts of voltage as the headboard banged against the wall.

"Okaaaaaaay! Okaaaaaaay!" he screamed.

I removed the torch from his leg. The horrible scent continued to fill the room.

"You need to talk to me. Tell me where my dad is," I said, fanning the smell of burnt flesh away from my face.

"Alright, alright, pah-leees, just don't burn me anymore."

"Mellow and Michael Thomson were behind it. I swear to God, I don't know where your father is."

"Wrong answer. You lie!"

I placed the torch on his leg again. That time, I looked at my Marc Jacobs watch as he released a bloodcurdling sound. One thing was for sure. I had all day.

I removed the torch from his inner thigh. I'd burned off a large section of flesh.

"Kadisha! I'll tell you! I'll tell you! Stop it! Stop it!" He writhed in excruciating pain.

"Talk, nigga. Next, it's your fucking balls and that skinny ass dick, muthafucka. I'm burning that bitch!" I spat.

"Oh, oh. It was me and Mellow and G, his cousin." Steve groaned in pain. For some reason, he was determined to keep Mellow's name in the mix. But at least he was now telling me half the truth, which was better than none.

"Why? Why did you do that to my family, my little sister and brother?" My bottom lip trembled. "Where is my father, and who put you up to this?"

"G asked me to do it. I needed the money. I was doin' bad."

"So, you did it. As good as my father has been to you?" Hurt and anger consumed me.

I felt all kinds of emotions, but none of them was sympathy. I placed the torch to his chest and burned off his nipple along with a part of his pec. He hollered so loud I was certain somebody had to have heard him.

"Shh! Shut up, punk ass nigga!" I hissed and snatched the pillowcase off his head.

I glanced at the window as a car's light flashed across the curtain. Somebody had pulled up in front of the room. I remained still. Then I asked, "How much money they give you? Tell me what's going on," I said and grabbed his dick. I placed the blow torch close enough for him to feel the heat. He began to talk a mile a minute.

"I think the Colombians put a hit out on your dad. I dunno. G was the go-between. He paid me ten stacks. They want the safe. They might have him stashed someplace if he is still alive," Steve said in one long breath as I looked down at his pathetic body.

The blow torch continued to roar in my hand as I tried to piece together what he said.

There was the safe and my father's abduction... But a Columbian drug lord? I thought, baffled, as I watched Steve squirm. What he had just told me was like a puzzle with all the major pieces missing. There were too many gaps, too many holes in his story. I didn't believe Steve.

"You lying!" I snatched his dick so hard that I felt something snap.

I was determined to make him tell me where my father was. I placed the torch to the head of his dick, lightly but enough to do serious damage. He screamed and bucked, struggling to get loose. The searing heat from the torch made the head bubble as it burned. He screamed like I was killing him, which I was.

Then, there was a knock at the door.

I pulled the blow torch away.

"Shhh, shut up! Be quiet!" I whispered to Steve.

Steve bucked his eyes and raised his head, craning his neck at the door. He looked at me like I was crazy, then looked back at the door as if considering his fate. Evidently, being alone with me holding a blow torch to his balls wasn't even an option. He opened his mouth wide.

"HELP MEEEEEE! HELP MEEEEE! SOMEBODY HELP MEEEEEE!" He screamed so loud it blew my hair back and hurt my ears.

With no other recourse, I popped his ass upside the head with the thick metal blow torch, knocking him out cold. Next, I crept over to the door with my heart racing in my chest. For some reason, it never occurred to me to put on some clothes. But I did pick up the gun.

As soon I peeked out the peephole, I damn near fainted at the two faces staring back at me. In the distance, I could see a lot of police helicopters in the sky. I heard a symphony of police cars' sirens blaring. I had no idea that Mellow was in a deadly shootout with G and his goons. The body count was high, more than any other city in America.

Leo Sullivan

Things quickly went from bad to worse.

CHAPTER Twenty-Seven

Kadisha

With no choice, I opened the door and let them in. They walked into the hotel room, making noise like a Miami hurricane.

"Uh, huh, bitch, you up to something—" Shamika was about to say as she and Latoya stormed into the hotel room.

She stopped mid-sentence and just looked at me, completely naked, with a gun in my hand. Then she sniffed the air, crinkled her nose, and scowled at me. The smell of burning flesh was awful.

"Girl, what is wrong with you?" she yelled.

I shut the door and heard Latoya scream as she backpedaled and almost tripped over a chair. She placed her hand over her mouth to stifle her scream and pointed at

Steve with the other hand. He was sprawled out naked on the bed with his thighs and chest tatted in horrific pink scars from the blow torch.

"Wha-da-fuck?!" Shamika gasped with her eyes bucked wide.

Latoya continued to scream.

"Bitch, shut up!" I said to Latoya, who was getting hysterical.

She looked between me and the gun. Instantly, tears streaked her face. Out of the three of us, she was the girly-girl. One hundred percent ultra-feminine and scary as hell.

"How did you know which room I was in?" I asked and resisted the urge to look out the window.

"Girl, Steve's car is parked right out front. Have you lost your fuckin' mind?!" Shamika screeched, with her eyes frantically looking around the room, then back at Steve.

I knew I must have looked like a deranged psycho bitch as their expressions started to hit home.

What the fuck am I doing? I asked myself and quickly tossed the thought out of my head. This was the path I'd chosen to avenge my family's tragedy and possibly find my father.

I blurted out, "I found out Steve was behind my family's home invasion. The whole thing. G put him up to it, but there is another mastermind involved, possibly a Columbian drug cartel," I said in a shaky voice and watched as Steve stirred, coming back to consciousness.

"Graylin Kelly's ass is next!" I added.

"Nawl, girl, you lying! You mean Graylin Kelly, known as G, the one that runs the John Doe Boys and is crazy as fuck? Him and Rah-Rah been going at it, bodies for bodies!"

I somberly nodded yes. Shamika and Rah-Rah used to mess around; she still had a crush on him and would let him hit it from time to time. She knew all about the beef between Rah-Rah and G, as well as the different cliques that had been murdering each other over drug turf. Shamika had an allegiance with Rah-Rah, like a ride-or-die chick. He was her dude, even though he was older than her. She was only twenty-one, and Rah-Rah was thirty with a gang of chicks he was sexing.

Shamika and Latoya both looked between Steve and me in disbelief. Suddenly, their facial expressions changed as it dawned on them what I'd said about Steve's involvement. Latoya and my sister Keona were tight. They would hang out at the mall together or go to football games to talk to boys.

"You need to beat his ass some more!" Latoya spitefully said.

Her jaw twitched as she narrowed her eyes at Steve, optic slants of hate. She then mumbled something under her breath and started looking around the room for something to hit him with.

"I knew Steve's ass wasn't right, and G, if he's got something to do with it, that's a major problem. That nigga and them John Doe niggaz done filled up two cemeteries with bodies. They don't even be playin', but he can't fuck with my dude Rah-Rah!" Shamika said while I put on my skirt and blouse.

Then, we heard a crash that startled us both. We turned around. Latoya had smashed the lamp over Steve's head and opened a big, nasty gash that was pouring blood.

"Girllll!!" Shamika and I both shrieked in unison.

"Keona was my girl," Latoya said with tears in her eyes.

Her actions choked me up. Again, I realized just how much I missed my little sister.

"Ohhhh, ohhhhh," Steve began to moan painfully.

"What you gon' do with him?" Shamika asked as she walked over to the bed where Steve was lying spread eagle.

"I'm going to make his ass tell me where my daddy is," I said as I picked up the blow torch and the cigarette lighter.

Shamika frowned.

Latoya stopped what she was doing. She had a Hennessey bottle poised in her hand, about to smash Steve over the head with it.

"I've been burning his ass with this torch."

"Uh, uh. You lying!" Latoya chimed in.

Phoof!

I lit the torch, and it roared like a baby inferno.

At the sound, Steve flinched, then suddenly woke up and stared at the dancing blue flame and the fiendish look in my eyes.

Crash!

"Naw! Bitch!" Latoya hit him over the head with the bottle, and the glass shattered.

Steve groaned in pain as more blood spewed from his head. I didn't even miss a beat. For some reason, having my girls with me helped in a way I couldn't explain. They validated my actions to seek revenge and find out where my daddy was. If that meant charbroiling Steve's ass for what he did and to make him talk, so be it.

I felt no remorse!

"Where is my daddy?" I asked and tried to ignore the quaver of emotions in my voice.

My hand with the blow torch was shaking as I stood over him. Shamika and Latoya watched with their mouths agape in riveting suspense.

"Pah-leees, Kadisha. I dunno where your father is! I'm sorry—"

"Wrong answer!" I said. Then, I placed the blowtorch to his balls and held it there. His nuts shriveled up and began to burn, making a frying sound like bacon. His screams for me to stop fell on deaf ears.

"Ohh, shit! Shit! Dayum, girl, you burned his nuts off. Look at that shit!" Shamika and Latoya both pointed as they hooted and hollered, jumping up and down in excitement.

The horrid smell of his flesh permeated the room. I fanned the air. A shoe came flying across the room and hit Steve in the face. Latoya was on the warpath again, hitting Steve with anything she could get her hands on.

The second time I pulled the torch away from him,

there was nothing left of his balls but crispy flesh that looked like a burned biscuit, black and smoldering.

I just happened to look over my shoulder, and stupid ass Latoya had her iPhone out, recording as Steve writhed in pain.

"Bitch, is you crazy?!" I yelled.

She frowned and placed the phone back into her purse. Steve continued to moan until he passed out again.

"Bingo!" Shamika exclaimed and pulled out two shoe boxes full of money and drugs from under the bed. There were at least two kilos of cocaine in one box. The other box was filled with cash.

"Oh, my god!" Latoya intoned with an astray in her hand that she was about to hit Steve with.

"Wow!" I said. I had a feeling that some of that money and drugs belonged to G and his crew, the John Doe Boys.

"Look at all this money and dope," Shamika said with her eyes sparkling.

"We splitting it down the middle," Latoya said, walking forward.

"Split shit, bitch. WE didn't find it. I did."

"Yes, we is splitting it!" I interjected.

Shamika looked at me and thought about objecting. She changed her mind after seeing the crazed look in my eyes as I held the blow torch, preparing to stick it to Steve again.

Just as I was about to place the torch to his face and wake his ass back up, Shamika grabbed my arm.

"Girl, I don't think he knows where your father is. Trust and believe if he knew, he would have told you by now. And this is probably not all Steve's money and dope, so we need to go."

"So, what you gon' do to him? He has seen all our faces," Latoya asked.

"Shit, we gotta kill him," Shamika said, holding the two shoe boxes stacked on top of each other. By her demeanor, I could tell she was ready to go.

I was, too. With ease, I picked the gun up off the floor. Neither of them had seen it. For some reason, Latoya's scary ass shirked away, grimacing as I placed the gun to Steve's head. Hesitating, a lot of memories flashed on the screen of my mind, some good, then bad. Memories of my sister lying in bed next to me getting raped and then shot, and the image of my little brother in the hospital.

I cocked the gun... Steve blinked and then opened his eyes. They were caked with blood. Just as I was getting ready to pull the trigger, Shamika hollered, "Nooo!"

"Whaat?!" I yelled. For some reason, my hand was shaking badly.

"Put the pillow over his head, so the gun don't make so much noise," she said.

She had a point. I placed the pillow over his head. He moved, struggling weakly as he began to suffocate. I looked over at Latoya. She was chowing down on her pink acrylic fingernails, watching me with heightened anticipation.

As I placed the gun to the pillow against his head, his legs continued to thrash around. I pulled the trigger.

Blocka!

All three of us nearly jumped out of our skin. That was when another car's lights flashed across the window curtains. Someone else had just pulled in front of the hotel room and quickly got out of their car.

"Oh, shit," Shamika said, looking out the window.

"What?"

Latoya just stood there, stuck on stupid, looking back and forth between the two of us.

"Tat-Tat and some dude coming this way!"

"You lying!" I yelled. My heart sank into my stomach like a pile of bricks.

"Help me untie him!" I yelled.

"For what!?"

"Just help me!" My voice cracked with desperation and fear. I didn't have to tell Latoya twice.

We untied Steve and shoved him off the bed onto the floor. I threw covers against the wall, concealing his body.

"They're coming this way and they got guns, some kind of rifle, an AK-47. She placed the shoe boxes down under the chair, took out her phone, and started texting. I heard a distinct sound like water running and looked over at Latoya. The sound was coming from her. Terrified, she was peeing down her leg on the carpet.

"I'm finna tell Rah-Rah dat G's dudes is here," Shamika said with her hands pecking away.

I suddenly had an idea to do the same. I took my phone out and started texting Mellow. Then, suddenly, the hotel door opened.

Too late!

To be continued....

www.ingramcontent.com/pod-product-compliance
Lightning Source LLC
Chambersburg PA
CBHW031944240626
47153CB00003B/860